Trey had only seconds to devise a plan.

Illuminated by the porch light, two men moved toward Macey's driveway, one carrying a body slung across his shoulder.

Macey. She wasn't trying to go on the run. She was being kidnapped.

He had one chance to salvage this mission. If he got anything wrong, Macey could vanish...or die.

Before he could take action, a series of galloping thuds stopped him and froze Macey's assailants. Her dog rounded the corner and leaped on one man, while Macey wrestled free from the other. Both men fled toward the van.

Macey jumped to go after them but Trey stopped her. "If you go near that van, you'll put yourself in worse danger."

"What just happened?" Her shoulders heaved up and down with her breaths.

The way she faced him told Trey she hadn't been running and his cover wasn't blown.

But the fight she'd waged against those men left him with questions. Questions he had to answer if he was going to prove her innocence...or put her in prison.

Jodie Bailey writes novels about freedom and the heroes who fight for it. Her novel *Crossfire* won a 2015 RT Reviewers' Choice Best Book Award. She is convinced a camping trip to the beach with her family, a good cup of coffee and a great book can cure all ills. Jodie lives in North Carolina with her husband, her daughter and two dogs.

Books by Jodie Bailey

Love Inspired Suspense

Freefall
Crossfire
Smokescreen
Compromised Identity
Breach of Trust
Dead Run
Calculated Vendetta
Fatal Response
Mistaken Twin
Hidden Twin
Canyon Standoff
"Missing in the Wilderness"
Fatal Identity
Under Surveillance

Texas Ranger Holidays

Christmas Double Cross

UNDER SURVEILLANCE

JODIE BAILEY

LOVE INSPIRED SUSPENSE
INSPIRATIONAL ROMANCE

LOVE INSPIRED® SUSPENSE
INSPIRATIONAL ROMANCE

ISBN-13: 978-1-335-40503-6

Recycling programs
for this product may
not exist in your area.

Under Surveillance

This edition published by arrangement with Harlequin Books S.A.

For questions and comments about the quality of this book, please contact us at CustomerService@Harlequin.com.

Love Inspired
22 Adelaide St. West, 40th Floor
Toronto, Ontario M5H 4E3, Canada
www.Harlequin.com

Printed in U.S.A.

Fear thou not; for I am with thee: be not dismayed;
for I am thy God: I will strengthen thee;
yea, I will help thee; yea, I will uphold thee
with the right hand of my righteousness.
—*Isaiah* 41:10

To all of you who prayed for Dad...
To all of you who continue to pray for Dad...
Thank you.

ONE

Macey Price muttered under her breath and stomped through damp leaves in the small wooded area behind her house. She brushed twigs out of her face in the rapidly deepening twilight. "Wait until I find that mutt." How in the world had he slipped out? He'd been in the house when she'd left for her run, hadn't he?

It didn't really matter. One street away from home, as Macey walked to cool down, Kito had come streaking past, galloping down a firebreak and alongside the edge of the woods. She'd tracked him along the wood line back toward the house. *Should have stayed on the road.* It would have been easier.

"One more time. One more Houdini escape and it's back to the rescue you came from." Okay, so she didn't really mean it. She'd sooner spend all of her evenings traipsing through the undergrowth calling Kito's name than give him up. The way that husky took off at the least squirrel or shadow was a small price to pay for his tail-wagging furry affection when he came home again an hour or so later.

An hour or so later, Macey stopped walking, ankle-deep in wet leaves and mud. When Kito decided to run, he always came back and either pawed at the front door or jumped the fence into Trey Burns's yard next door. This woods walk was pointless. She angled up the slight hill to dry ground and followed privacy fences along the back of the houses on her street. She'd take the shower she desperately needed after her planned post-work jog and her unplanned tromp through the swampy woods, then eat dinner on the deck so she could keep an eye on Trey's yard.

When her roommate had brought the dog home two years ago, training the willful pup had been a beast. Olivia's frequent work trips had made Kito feel more like Macey's dog anyway. She'd actually inherited Kito when Olivia died in a car accident in Italy two months ago.

No, she really wouldn't trade him.

As she rounded the Jacksons' privacy fence, her brick ranch came into view. Macey opened her mouth to call one more time, just in case Kito had doubled back, but something stilled her feet and her words.

A beam of light moved across the glass door that led from the elevated deck into her dining room.

Someone was in her house.

Instinctively, Macey dropped to one knee, seeking feeble cover behind her split-rail-and-chicken-wire fence. She dared not move, dared not breathe as her heart picked up past double time. Her teeth clamped into her lower lip so tightly she should have tasted blood. Soggy leaves soaked damply through the knee of her leggings. She needed her phone. Maybe even a really big stick. Something.

Another beam passed across the windows in Olivia's bedroom. She swallowed hard against a rising tide of bile. No one had been in that room since the call that Olivia had died. Now at least two intruders were walking through Macey's home and likely digging through her things, searching...taking.

Far from scared, she was angry. Violated. Determined. There had to be something she could do to stop this.

Macey glanced around in the rapidly darkening twilight, searching for a way to fight back. She hadn't taught self-defense in college for nothing.

The back of her property sat on high ground, dropping off quickly at the back. The house to her left was empty since the Jacksons were on an early fall trip to Disney World. Trey Burns lived on the other side, but his house had been dark since he'd gone on a field exercise with his unit two days earlier. The reason she was keeping an eye on his place. And the reason she was on her own.

The smart thing would be to slip back the way she'd come. It would be easy to edge back through the trees to the neighbor who shared her back woods and call 9-1-1 from there.

But by the time the police arrived, everything she owned could be gone. Shucking off the reflective jacket she wore when she ran, Macey tossed it aside and prepared to slip closer to the house. Maybe her appearance would scare them off.

But the back door to the deck flew open and a man stepped outside. A bulky silhouette in the near darkness, he swung the beam of a high-powered flashlight across the backyard, concentrating close to the house at first, then sweeping in ever-widening arcs toward the fence. Macey hunkered lower. Suddenly, facing huge men by herself didn't seem like such a good idea. *God, don't let him spot me.* Prayer wasn't her usual go-to, but now seemed like a good time to start.

A second man joined him on the deck, invisible behind the light he swung in a crisscross over the first man's. "Can't find anything inside." The voice was low but it hung heavy in the damp evening air, his Deep South accent drawling the words thick and slow. The words sent a chill along Macey's arms, turning post-run sweat into cold, clammy fear.

"Want to take the girl if she comes back? Wasn't the plan but might as well bring them something instead of nothing."

These men were looking for quick cash by any means necessary, even if it meant— Macey clamped her hand over her mouth. She couldn't get sick. She wouldn't.

"Sure. You wait in the house. I'll cover outside." One light vanished as the door closed, while the second man lumbered down the deck stairs, flashlight searching as he moved.

Her breath caught in her throat, nearly strangling her. Split rails and chicken wire gave her no cover. If he came this way and scanned the woods…

A crash in the dry leaves drew a gasp from Macey and a cry from the man hunting her. She pressed her full body into the damp ground, hoping Kito wouldn't give away her position. Hoping the man wouldn't see her.

Hoping for somebody, somewhere, to rescue her from a situation she'd never imagined in her worst nightmares.

Kito streaked from the dark woods behind the Jacksons' house, then veered to the right toward the creek, probably on the trail of an unsuspecting cat. Macey had always been fond of stray cats, but never so much as in that moment, when one lured her dog from danger.

The husky might be safe, but when Macey lifted her head from the damp leaves, the beam of light bounced across the ground in front of her and reflected off her jacket only a few feet away. Why hadn't she thrown it farther?

The light swung back, footsteps pounded and a shout followed. Heart hammering in every pore of her body, Macey abandoned all pretense of hiding, scrambled to her feet and ran into the woods.

If she could only scream for help, but no words would come out of her dry mouth. There wasn't enough oxygen to power her body and release a cry.

She heard a thud. Her pursuer must have jumped the fence to tear after her through the underbrush. He might be faster, but thanks to Kito's frequent wandering, she knew these woods. If she could keep this pace for the half mile through the swamp to the main road, she'd be safe. Surely no one would hurt her in front of witnesses.

The man behind her crashed closer until she could hear his hard breathing and his fingertips brushed the back of her shirt. More. She needed more.

His fingers grasped her shirt and he jerked her to a halt.

Her head whipped back and hit her attacker's cheek,

shooting painful stars across her vision as he yanked her off her feet.

With a violent yank, he twisted and threw her face-down to the ground, pinning her with a knee between her shoulder blades.

Macey struggled, dead leaves and mud sliding against her cheek and forcing their way into her mouth. She gagged.

The man dug his knee in harder, grinding her spine until she whimpered and went limp, the pain too blinding to fight.

After pulling her arms behind her back, he hefted himself up, then yanked her to her feet. The motion nearly ripped her shoulders from their sockets, bringing instant numbness into her fingers. He leaned closer, his breath hot on her cheek. "You shouldn't have run." He twisted her arm tighter against her back. "Would have been easier if you hadn't run." The hard press of steel dug into her spine. "I wouldn't suggest doing it again."

Macey didn't let her shoulders fall, not even with a gun to her back. No matter that her insides quivered and quaked, she couldn't show fear. She had to stay strong, to look for an opportunity. She had years of self-defense training behind her, and though she might be rusty, she sure wasn't weak.

The hard part would be waiting for the right moment when all she wanted was to fight now, harder than she ever had before. She had to trust her training.

Her feet stumbled as her captor shoved her toward the house, but she righted herself and kept going, refusing to speak. As long as she was silent, her voice wouldn't tremble and give away the fear that coursed through her. She had to appear stoic; any sign of weakness would give this guy and his partner the upper hand.

The man practically hauled her over the fence, then half dragged her across the yard. By the front fence at the corner of the house, he shoved her against the brick wall, pinning her there with the back of her neck. He peeked around the corner to survey the area.

Her assailant turned to her, his ice-blue eyes too close. He scanned her face and seemed to search for something in her expression. His focus was cold and menacing. "You're too quiet. Makes me wonder what's going on in that head of yours." He jabbed the gun into her ribs, and she fought a gasp. "Just don't get to thinking that smart can outrun a bullet." His baritone voice scraped against her ear. It held the frightening darkness of deep woods, violent sports and too much whiskey. Like her father before he'd left.

As he leaned around the corner again, the pressure on her neck eased. The gun slipped to the right.

Now.

Macey threw her free hand up and caught the man's wrist. The gun clattered against the house.

As he turned toward her, she thrust out her palm and caught him square in the nose. A horrific crunch followed the blow as blood streamed down his face.

The man roared and grabbed his face.

Macey shoved him backward to the ground and scrambled over the fence, heading for the street. Someone had to be home on her cul-de-sac. Someone had to help her.

She rounded the corner of the house and collided with another man. He pressed his hand against her mouth, wrapped his arm around her waist and then dragged her toward a van idling in her drive.

Get Macey Price. Now.

For months, Trey Blackburn had been sitting on "go," battling a surge of adrenaline every time a new text message chimed. Today the command to move had finally come. Whatever intel his team had received from others in the network, it was serious enough to break his cover and demanded he move quickly.

If he wasn't already too late.

In his infantry days, he'd been on call for missions that hadn't revved his adrenaline this high. The engine of his pickup fought to race under his foot, but he couldn't risk flying through the small neighborhood of houses built on large wooded lots. Still, the tires barely hugged the road when he whipped past his cul-de-sac and spotted a white construction van in Macey Price's driveway.

The sight made his heart pound even harder. His fingers itched to call for backup, but there was none. With his team based in the mountains of North Carolina, he was the sole member undercover several hours away at Fort Bragg. The police would be a big help, but mission security dictated he maintain anonymity. So against his better judgment, he resisted the urge to dial 9-1-1. It was up to him to take Macey Price into custody if she was about to flee. And it looked like she might have accomplices.

Maintaining speed to keep from scaring his suspects into doing something stupid, Trey pulled into the driveway of a house for sale on the neighborhood's main street. He shut off the engine, shoved the flashlight from his glove box into his back pocket and walked around the side of the house as though nothing was wrong. It took everything in him not to run for Macey's house, but doing so without recon could be deadly. Still, time was short and he had to move quickly.

Whatever Macey Price was into, whomever the bad guys were that she was dealing with, something had apparently snapped and they'd decided to make a move. She'd given no indication the day before that anything was wrong. She'd treated his undercover persona just like she always had as they'd watched hockey while snacking on pizza. If she was truly guilty, she was very good at deception.

Once he gained the rear of the vacant house, he doubled back, crossed the road and slipped through side yards to his own backyard. The cover of soft darkness in the damp evening brought a short breath of gratitude. In the same thought, he was glad for the pistol at his hip, even though he desperately hoped he wouldn't have to use it.

He crept closer, watching that van, but there was no motion around it. If Macey was packing up to bolt, she was taking her time. Or it could be something worse. If she was already in the vehicle, he'd failed in his mission because she would vanish, likely forever.

There was no counting the ways he'd pay for that kind of mistake. If Macey was truly guilty and she escaped, the case the government had been building for nearly a year against shadowy figures stealing military intelligence would crumble between his fingers.

But if she was innocent, the way he was beginning to suspect, then the danger was even more grave.

At the corner of his house, Trey's feet sank into the grass. He waited for any sound from next door before he peeked around the corner. Voices, low and angry, drifted through the early evening darkness from near the driveway.

Trey slipped around the corner and stayed close to brick still warm from the sun, edging closer to Macey's house as he plotted a strategy. From the sound of it, there were only two men helping Macey, unless more were hiding somewhere. It was a risk Trey had to take.

Illuminated in the porch light, two men were moving toward Macey's driveway, one carrying a body slung across his shoulder.

Macey. She wasn't trying to run. She was being kidnapped.

He shouldn't feel an emotional drop in his stomach at the thought she might be hurt. Not now. Not under any circumstances, actually. But he did.

He'd unpack that later. At the moment, he had one chance to salvage this mission, but only if he acted now. The way he figured it, the clock offered him two seconds to assess the situation and do everything right the first time.

If he got even one thing wrong, then Macey could vanish or die while some seriously bad dudes would get away with murder. Multiple murders.

The element of surprise would—

A crash and a series of galloping thuds from the side yard of Macey's house stopped Trey in his thoughts and movements.

It froze Macey's assailants, too.

What in the world?

The scene spun into motion all at once. Kito bounded around the corner and didn't hesitate to join in what any playful husky would see as fun and games. He leaped on the man closest to Trey's position, staggering him backward.

In the same moment, Macey grabbed the belt of the man carrying her and pulled upward. As he lurched forward from the sudden movement, she leveraged her body weight. Kicking her legs to free them, she slid headfirst down the man's back to the ground, where she rolled to a standing position. She whirled and rushed her off-balance attacker, shoving him to his knees.

Trey didn't dwell on how impressed he was by the move. He hustled into the fray with an unintelligible shout, heading for the other terrified man who seemed to believe the friendly, jumping husky was trying to kill him.

Before he got there, both men scrambled to their feet and ran for the idling van.

Macey jumped to go after them, but Trey reached her first and grabbed the back of her shirt, hauling her backward against his chest. "If you get near that van, you'll put yourself in worse danger."

She moved to attack him but stopped at his words, likely recognizing his voice. Her muscles visibly tensed as the van screeched out of her driveway and roared out of the cul-de-sac. When it disappeared, she whirled on him, wrenching the back of her running shirt from his grasp. "What just happened?" Her shoulders heaved up and down with her breaths. "And where did you come from?"

The way she faced him and the questions she asked told Trey everything he needed to know. Clearly, Macey Price hadn't been running and his cover hadn't been blown.

But the fight she'd waged against those men and the innocence of her asks left Trey with questions of his own. Questions he had to answer if he was going to prove her innocence...or put her in prison.

TWO

Macey closed the door behind the police officer, then dropped onto the dark brown leather sofa while her mother puttered in the kitchen, probably trying to see what was happening out the back window.

It was truly impossible that her evening had gone down the way it had. What kind of idiot was she, considering a toe-to-toe with two armed men who'd broken into her house?

Looking for what? As far as she could tell, nothing was missing, although several rooms were a complete train wreck. But her laptop still sat on the dining room table on the other side of the living room. The drawer where she stashed extra cash hung open in the kitchen, but the money was still there. Her tablet still rested on her nightstand in her bedroom up the hallway.

It made zero sense.

She shut her eyes as a tremor started deep in her stomach and worked its way out until even her teeth rattled. Strange men. In her house. Men who'd grabbed her, had tried to shove her into a van…

A weight rested on her knee, followed by a heavy canine sigh.

Kito.

Cracking one eye open, Macey leaned forward and rested her forehead against the dog's, burying her fingers in the thick gray-and-white fur around his neck. Calm washed over her. The dog might be a wide-open ball of energy with a boundless need to explore, but he always seemed to know when she needed a little bit of love to make everything better. "You're the best in the world, aren't you, buddy?" She whispered the endearment and he dipped his head between her knees, letting her scratch his ears.

Yeah, he really was the best. Her recently deceased roommate might have rescued the dog from a shelter, but the dog had definitely rescued Macey more than once. It might be cliché, but it was true.

"You okay, honey?" Her mother approached and sat beside her on the couch. She set a glass of water on the coffee table, then leaned over and scratched between Kito's ears. "You've said over and over again that huskies aren't guard dogs, but you might be wrong. He sure got the job done today, I hear."

"He's not a guard dog at all. Huskies don't bark and couldn't care less about random noises. He was welcoming the bad guys to the neighborhood, asking them to be his friends. That's what he does best. Just so happened his new buddies weren't all that interested in making his acquaintance." Kito's stature, coloring and piercing blue eyes made him a fearsome-looking animal. But, like most huskies, he was way too friendly to care about being an attack dog, even when the situation called for it.

Macey patted his side to let him know cuddle time was over, then sat back on the couch. She wanted to lay her head on her mother's shoulder and find some measure of comfort, but it would only be an illusion. Her mother had never been one to put her daughter first. She was only here now because there was drama to be witnessed.

Still, it would be nice to have a mom who looked at her instead of through her, one who truly put her daughter first for once.

It would never happen.

Kito trotted off to watch out the front storm door, where Trey was still talking to one of the responding officers near her front porch. While most people seemed a little stiff when they spoke to the police, Trey's stance was relaxed. Well, his arms were crossed, but in that casual way of his. Maybe he knew the guy. Maybe it was because he was in the military and was still wearing his uniform. Or maybe they were talking about hockey scores and the conversation had nothing to do with her home being invaded.

Another shudder quaked in her chest. *My home being—*

"He's definitely pretty, isn't he?" Her mom had leaned forward and was following Macey's gaze out the front window.

"Kito?" Macey's voice shook. She swallowed to try to bring it back under control.

"No. Trey."

And…tremor halted with a jolt. Good thing she

hadn't been drinking any of that water her mother had brought for her. "What? Mom, really?"

Shoving a lock of brunette hair behind her ear, Tiffany Price shrugged. "I never said I wanted to date him. Just that he's—"

"Okay. Enough." Shoving up from the couch, Macey paced to the fireplace and faced the back door so Trey was out of her line of sight. Kicked in by the robbers, the door hung open on its hinges, the wood frame near the lock splintered. This was the very reason she couldn't even begin to think about what her mother was saying.

Besides, Trey was... Well, Trey was her neighbor. Her friend. They watched football together. And hockey. He'd never shown a speck of interest in her outside of that. To consider making their relationship anything else was ridiculous.

Although, she couldn't deny her mother was telling the truth. At a little over six feet tall, with light brown hair cut short but not too short, blue eyes and a military-bred stature... Okay, so she wouldn't choose the word *pretty*. He was beyond that word.

And she shouldn't be noticing. According to him, his job with the army made it hard to build a relationship. The way he talked, he was probably with some covert Special Forces unit. Also, he'd hinted at some hurt in his past that he'd never explained. Still, she'd noticed how female heads turned when she was with him.

Macey glanced to the side. Her mom sat on the couch, eyeing her with a knowing smile.

What her mother thought she knew was beyond her. There was nothing between Trey Burns and Macey except friendship. Never would be. She'd learned from a walkaway father and a distracted mother that romantic relationships weren't worth the effort or the heartbreak. "Let's just leave the word *pretty* off the table, okay?"

"Who's pretty?" A deeper voice, definitely not her mother's, stiffened her shoulders as the glass door clicked shut on the other side of the living room.

Seriously. He had to walk in for that part?

"Clint Eastwood when he was younger," her mother answered before Macey could.

Wow. Smooth. But what else had she expected? Macey turned to face Trey, dragging herself back to reality, to what had happened and to why they were all in her living room when it was getting dangerously close to what was normally her bedtime. "What are the police planning to do?"

Trey strode into the room and dropped into the recliner. "As much as they can. I gave them access to the footage from my doorbell camera, but I don't know if it will do any good. This is going to be a slow process that may not yield a lot of results if they can't find any fingerprints or witnesses other than the two of us." He shifted in the seat and the leather creaked. "You being assaulted bumps the priority level up from your average home invasion, though."

Assaulted. The word was ugly and jagged, ripping along the nerves she'd so far managed to hold together. It was a crime show word. A prime-time news word. A horror movie word. It was not a word that should ever apply to her.

Macey wrapped her arms around her stomach and willed it to stop shaking. She couldn't fall apart in front of her mother and Trey. It would be humiliating. Before she became a physical therapist, she'd taught countless women how to defend themselves. While her instincts hadn't failed her, her emotions had. Never once in all of those years of teaching self-defense had she considered the mental toll an attack would take. No doubt, when everyone left, she was going to curl up in the shower and cry the ugly cry.

"Mace…" Trey sat forward in the chair, resting his elbows on his knees. "It's okay to be scared. What happened tonight was—"

"What happened tonight is over. And I need it to be over so I can get it shoved behind me and stop thinking about it." So she could feel safe in her own home again. So she could fall asleep without flying apart at every little sound. She didn't want to live that way, but the likelihood was high that she would for a long time.

And she hated those men for it.

What if Olivia had lived to experience the fear that now coursed through Macey? What if Olivia had been home when they'd broken in? Sure, Macey had taught her some skills, at Olivia's request, but would she have been able to save herself?

Then again, if Olivia was still alive, they'd have each other to lean on as they'd had before in several tough times since becoming roommates and best friends. Olivia. Her room had suffered the brunt of the invasion. Macey hated the men for that, too.

"You have to live it for a little while." Her mom cast a glance at Trey, then crossed her legs as though she was trying to be casual, although Macey knew better. She was antsy to get out of there now that the excitement had died down. "Eventually there will be more questions. More investigation. Like Trey said, the police aren't done yet."

Macey closed her eyes and pulled in a deep breath. Couldn't they just stop talking? Let it go? Let her have five minutes of denial?

"Speaking of questions…" It was Trey this time. "Any idea what they might have been looking for?"

"None." Trey had walked through the house with her after the police had given their okay, trying to help her catalog missing items. "They were leaving when I came up on them. It doesn't look like they'd been here long. I went for my run and saw Kito on the next street over when I returned. He must have gotten out when they came in. I followed him along the wood line, and you were involved in what happened after that." She raised her hands helplessly. Trey knew the rest, and she didn't particularly want to rehash how she'd gone all Rambo on two men outside of her house. Not in front of her mother, anyway.

"No big ATM withdrawals recently? No bonuses at work? No unexpected financial windfall someone might have found out about?"

Macey arched her eyebrow. "That's a lot of focus on money, Trey. Do you know something I don't?" She forced a grin to let him know she was trying to be funny and then shook her head. "I stuff most of my money into savings, so, for the most part, I'm a paycheck-to-paycheck kind of girl. Besides, work's not in a position to be offering up extra money." As part of a small independent clinic in the shadow of a larger hospital system that tended to take up all of the business, her job as a physical therapist didn't exactly rake in the big bucks.

He didn't smile. "Just concerned. Break-ins in this neighborhood are rare. We're on an out-of-the-way cul-de-sac. Seems a little too weird to be random."

"The fact that your houses are tucked out of the way might be exactly why they came here." Her mom shot a warning look at Trey. It was a level of disapproval she rarely showed him. She'd hinted almost since the day he'd moved in that Macey might want to consider him as husband material. "Less chance of being seen. You might want to consider—" Her mother reached for her phone, which lay facedown on the coffee table, and read the screen. She smiled briefly and angled it so that Macey couldn't see her phone.

Macey turned away. Whatever that text was, it was going to pull her mother away. Now that the drama had passed and her mother had a good story to tell her friends, she'd be off to something else. Something that didn't include her daughter.

Rolling her eyes to the ceiling, Macey counted to ten. She was only worthy of attention until something better came along.

"That was Kim." There was a rustle as her mother gathered her purse and coat from the couch. "There's a group getting together at her house in half an hour to watch the two-hour episode of that new dating show. Looks like a good one."

Steeling herself, Macey turned and faced her mother. "Have fun." Her voice stayed level, the tone contrary to the words.

Trey looked away.

"Now, Macey…" Her mother paused with her purse dangling from her fingers. "You're clearly safe and you don't need me anymore. Those men are long gone, and you'll probably start cleaning up as soon as I leave. You don't need me for that."

"You're right. Go." Yeah, it was all bravado. She'd learned long ago that wanting her mom would only lead to disappointment.

"Don't worry about Macey, Mrs. Price." Trey stepped closer. "I'll walk you out, grab a couple of things from my house, and then I'm planning to help Macey clean up. I'll bunk on her couch tonight. She'll be fine. I—"

"Bunk on my couch?" Sure, he was at the house enough to practically be another roommate, but he'd never spent the night under the same roof. No way did Macey intend to let him start now.

Even if the idea of his presence did clamp the lid on some of her fears.

With a smile, her mother dropped a kiss on Macey's cheek before she turned to Trey. "That's good to hear, Trey. She doesn't need me at all when she has you." She didn't look back as she walked out the door, Trey in her wake.

When the door shut behind them, Macey stretched her arms out to the sides and turned her face to the ceiling. What had she expected? In the end, even her own mother couldn't be counted on to stand beside her.

"So she threw herself into the fray and tried to fight off two men breaking into her house? Single-handedly? And unarmed?" On Trey's laptop screen, his team's commander, Captain Gavin Harrison, whistled low and his eyebrows tented. One of the original recruits to the army's investigative unit dubbed Eagle Overwatch, Harrison was no-nonsense when it came to their mission, but his sense of humor always shone through. In a job like theirs, it had to. "That's some bold stuff. If she wasn't a credible suspect in this whole espionage ring, I'd say we hire her."

Suspect. Trey stopped pacing and dropped into the chair at his desk, facing his computer. In the craziness and confusion, he'd nearly forgotten that Macey Price very much *was* a suspect in a yearlong investigation into government contractors allegedly stealing secrets and selling them on the dark web to the highest bidder. Worse, evidence strongly indicated that Macey was dealing to Sapphire Skull, an upstart domestic terrorism organization led by Jeffrey and Adrian Frye. A couple of low-level punks looking to make a name for themselves, the Frye brothers had certainly found a way to do it.

With government employees involved and no way to tell how deep the conspiracy ran, Criminal Investigations had called on Eagle Overwatch, a deep-cover investigative military team, to deal with long-term surveillance.

Trey had spent months undercover, befriending Macey and her roommate, Olivia, trying to gain their trust. All evidence had indicated that one of the women was the ringleader, though figuring out which one had eluded them. Until her death, Olivia had seemed the likeliest, given her job as a government contractor, but Trey hadn't yet been able to clear Macey. A trail of emails and bank drafts seemed to indicate she was brokering intel, but where would she obtain classified information without Olivia to help her?

An even larger issue loomed, one he'd discussed with Captain Harrison on more than one occasion. Macey presented none of the indicators of a person dealing with criminals. He'd dealt with thieves and liars in the past, and Macey wasn't like any of them.

Brown-haired, brown-eyed Macey. Who worked with patients in a private clinic as a physical therapist. Who'd forced him to watch that *Princess Bride* movie so many times even he could quote it. Who made a mean homemade pizza crust and—

"You with me, Blackburn?" The captain's pointed question cut through his thoughts.

"Yeah. I'm here." It didn't matter what good things Macey was. She was a suspect first and foremost. If she was guilty, she deserved jail for treason.

A harsh word. A harsher reality. One his emotions had no business in.

But he couldn't deny that the longer he was around her, the more he believed she was innocent in spite of the evidence. A horrible trait in an investigator.

Captain Harrison eyed him through the camera, then seemed to adjust his thinking. "So our intel was good that these guys were about to move, only they weren't on the move *with* Macey Price. They were on the move to *locate* her, possibly to harm her. That adds a whole new dimension to this investigation. We need to find out exactly who they are."

"They can't stay ghosts forever. They'll slip up eventually." And when they did, Macey would either be proved innocent…or she'd be a notorious name on in-

ternational news. "Here's the deal… Macey seemed
genuinely clueless. The way she talks, this was random to her. She showed no indication that she knew
what they were after, no nervous tics when it came to
the police being in her house. Nothing."

"Hmm. Either Macey Price is the slickest of liars—"

"Or she's innocent."

"Look, I know this isn't easy." Harrison scratched
his chin and sat back in his desk chair. Even though it
was late, he was still at Eagle Overwatch's headquarters
at Camp McGee near Mountain Springs, North Carolina. Ostensibly a small training post, the remote location made McGee the ideal place to host the deep-cover
unit. "It's hard to walk that line between suspect and
friend. It can get blurry really fast."

"It's not blurry." Trey's defenses crept up and the
words held a snap he didn't usually employ when talking to a superior. He knew what his job was, and he
wasn't going to fail. Macey Price was a suspect, plain
and simple. Nothing more.

Harrison's lip crept into a half smile. "You sure about
that?"

"I'm sure. It's just tedious when there isn't any new
evidence to point to her. All we have is some old emails
and some old bank transactions that anyone could have
planted. She's been squeaky clean the whole time I've
been here."

"And yet…"

"And yet the evidence can't be denied, either."

A tip from a credible source that Macey was involved… A trip to Denver that coincided with one of
the sales… An offshore bank account that regularly

received sizable deposits they had yet to successfully trace… Late-night cell phone calls from her phone to random burner phones, all lining up with data thefts… The stack of evidence against Macey was high.

But the government was being cautious before it swooped in. If Overwatch moved too soon, the bad guys could be spooked into hiding, and the government wanted the one linchpin who held it all together. Trey's team needed concrete proof linking those phone calls and Macey's trip to active buyers from the government's watch list. So far, there just wasn't enough.

"Well, now you have some action to work with. Someone was definitely snooping in her house, and she knew exactly how to take down the threat. With her bare hands, no less."

Trey nodded, his lips a tight line. "She taught self-defense in college, so there's no surprise she was able to get out of that situation. When it comes to solid proof, we're still in the gray."

"Tonight you've got a really good crack at getting some answers," Harrison said. "If you're going over there to help her clean up the mess they left behind, then you'll have access to a lot of spaces you don't normally have access to."

It was the upside of a bad situation. He'd been able to do a limited amount of surface-level searching when he'd been at the house but had been unable to do any real inside digging alone. When Olivia was alive, she'd set up a seriously complicated security system, and the team had been cautious about gaining entry to the house. They needed to keep court orders and such on the down-low while still operating under legal authority so that when they were ready to present a case, nothing would be thrown out on a technicality. With Macey giving him permission to "help" her tonight, Trey could definitely scope out new intel.

"Also, given that this is amping up, I'm sending Staff Sergeant Richardson and Dana Santiago to you. They should be there late tomorrow or early the next day. My gut says this is about to blow wide-open and you don't need to be out there alone."

"Sir, I—"

"I've got the rest of our team and a backup security detail headed your way," Harrison said. "We need eyes on Macey Price at all times, so you can switch shifts with them. I want her going to work and living her life as normal so we can keep your cover safe. They'll watch her when you can't. Richardson can provide backup at your house, and Dana will be available to dig into any tech you can get your hands on."

Trey bristled. Did the team commander not trust him? After all this time? "I think I—"

"This is not about trust, Blackburn. I feel like the endgame is coming, that we're close to something big. This isn't about you."

"Yes, sir." Sure, it made sense, but Trey's past still reared up with the sting of a hornet. He'd probably never feel good enough or trusted enough.

"Here's a thought." Captain Harrison's chair creaked through the speakers as he shifted and sat straight again. "You said she seemed rattled by the home invasion and clueless as to why it was happening to her. It's definitely interesting to me that she'd give you as much access to the house as she's offering up right now. If she was truly a woman with something to hide…"

Then she'd never let anyone get as close as she had let—and was about to let—Trey get.

Trey sighed. "It could be she's just that good."

"You do realize investigation isn't just about guilt. We have an obligation to protect the innocent as well as to bring the guilty to justice. You have to keep an open mind to both sides. Facts. You're searching for facts."

"I know that."

"And *I* know that your past tends you toward expecting the worst of people, even the ones who seem the most innocent."

Trey bristled. His personal life was off the table and Captain Harrison knew that very well. "I also learned a long time ago that you can never trust a criminal. Sometimes the nicest, most innocent people turn out to be the ones who have eight bodies in the basement freezer." He shuddered. "And on that note, I'm heading next door. If she's hiding anything, I don't want her to have too much time to move it." Facts might be facts, but it was hard not to let his instincts join in on the game.

"Roger that. You be careful."

"Aren't I always?" Trey held his finger over the laptop's trackpad, ready to disconnect. "Know what? Don't answer that." He killed the video call in the middle of the team commander's chuckle. His propensity for not staying safe was what had landed him in Gavin Harrison's sights in the first place and his eventual assignment to Eagle Overwatch.

He'd never dreamed his first long-term undercover op would linger for so many months.

Or that a case he'd initially thought would be laid out in stark black and white would fall into so many variations of gray.

THREE

Macey stood in the doorway of her bedroom and dug her teeth into her bottom lip. It was the only room in the house that hadn't been touched. In every other area, chaos ruled the day. But in here? She must have surprised them before they'd gotten as far as her most personal space. It was an odd calm in the middle of a raging sea.

Kito leaned against her leg, probably sensing her distress. He hadn't left her side since her mother and Trey had walked out the front door, frequently pressing his whole weight against her. While he tended to fight formal training, it turned out he was a pretty good emotional support animal.

Absently, Macey scratched the spot between his ears. Her pristine room ought to make her feel slightly less violated. Instead it creeped her out, as if her home was a job the criminals had left unfinished and would be back to complete.

She shuddered at the thought. A tap on the front door nearly sent her running for the shattered back door. Grabbing the bedroom door frame to keep her balance as her socked feet slid on the hardwood, she pressed her hand to her chest.

Kito bounced for the front door, always happy for more company.

Wild dog. Macey took a deep, steadying breath and tried to center her thoughts. It was probably Trey. It was about time for him to return. He'd promised to fix the back door and to help her clean up.

After padding up the short hallway, Macey headed across the living area to let him in, prepared to argue her earlier point. While she was grateful for his help and would let him stay as long as he wanted to lend a hand with setting everything back to rights, she wasn't about to let him spend the night on her couch.

That seemed a little beyond what their usual friend-ship was. She unlocked the dead bolt and yanked the door open. His presence was unnecessary, too. Surely those men would not be foolish enough to come back. They'd likely look somewhere else. Somewhere with a less stringent security system.

A less stringent security system.

She stopped with her hand on the storm door's lock. Before she'd left the house to go for her run, she'd set the alarm. How had it not gone off when the men had kicked in her back door?

"What?" Trey's voice cut through the glass door and the paralysis that had smacked her. "Mace? You going to let me in or stand there staring at me?"

Shaking her head, she twisted the bolt and let Trey in, then locked the storm door behind him. She shut the front door and turned the dead bolt. She wanted both sealed against invisible threats outside.

Maybe she wouldn't mind so much if Trey spent his night camped on her couch after all.

He settled a small duffel bag and a toolbox on the floor by the door, then squeezed past her into the living room, stopping to rub his knuckles over Kito's head. "You okay?" he asked her. "I literally just watched you turn white."

"Why didn't the house alarm go off?" She didn't turn to face him, just stared at the back of her front door, her racing thoughts finally getting the better of her.

"Are you sure you set it?" His voice came from over her shoulder, close by, close enough for his presence to be felt against her back. "You were headed out for your run. Maybe you forgot? Maybe you meant to and got distracted by Kito?"

With a sigh, Macey turned and brushed past Trey, walking into the kitchen and to the keypad installed by the garage door.

Kito followed and slurped water from his dish, the everyday sound grating on Macey's nerves. She stared at the keypad. The system was bulky and overcomplicated, one Olivia had designed and installed when she'd moved in several years ago. "I never set the whole system, just the doors and windows. All of that stuff Olivia had turned on was too much. But I definitely remember pressing in the code this evening. My finger slipped on the last key when Kito came tearing around the corner and hit my knee, so I had to wipe out the code and start over."

"Maybe you didn't fully set it? Maybe Kito threw you off?"

"Maybe." At this point, Macey doubted everything about her own memories and her own actions. She'd fallen down the rabbit hole, had witnessed her home being invaded and had engaged in a physical altercation with thugs all by herself. Maybe she should go to bed in her untouched room and pretend the rest of the house was pristine and peaceful.

Trey stepped up to her side and tapped the digital screen on the alarm system. "This is a fairly safe neighborhood. I never did understand why Olivia insisted on such an overkill alarm."

In spite of herself, Macey snorted a chuckle. "Same. We went round and round over it after I set it off several times. She went all out with the motion sensors and the pressure pads in the floor, and I'm pretty sure there are heat sensors somewhere. Even cameras on the doors. She was paranoid."

"Why?"

"Said she saw a lot of things working in intelligence, including the worst side of humanity. Claimed that, without the alarm set, she'd lie awake at night convinced someone was coming in the back door to annihilate humanity with our house as ground zero." Actually, that wasn't as funny now as it used to be.

"She never struck me as the paranoid type."

Macey shrugged. "Since she—" She inhaled deeply and exhaled slowly. *Since she died.* Two months later and it was still hard to believe her best friend was truly gone. Two months ago, she'd left for a work trip and died in a car accident in Italy. The phone call from Olivia's aunt was burned forever into her mind.

Macey shook off the memory. "Anyway, Olivia designed the whole thing herself, but I got into the computer that runs the system and shut down pretty much everything except the doors and windows. I can just see myself getting up for water in the middle of the night and having some net fall on my head like an old Bugs Bunny cartoon."

"Man, I hope there aren't nets in the ceiling. That would be a little much." Trey tapped Macey on the shoulder. "Come on. I'm going to piece your door frame back together and reinforce it for tonight. I'll need an extra hand to do it. After that, we can get started on this mess. Tomorrow we can go buy you a new one."

Exhaustion descended on Macey like a cold, wet blanket. "I don't know. Maybe we just put the door back together and then call it a night. It's almost midnight, and you have to work tomorrow."

"I took the day off. You need help and I've got some leave to burn up, and since we just came out of the field, now seems like a good time for a break." He wrapped an arm around her shoulders and pulled her close in a quick, brotherly hug. "Trust me. You won't sleep tonight if you know this mess is out here. I know you. You can be a little…" He drew away and raised an eyebrow.

"A little what?" She shoved him in the shoulder, genuinely amused at his teasing. Maybe she did need him around after all. "A little too much of a neat freak? A little too much like Monica on *Friends*?"

"You said it. I didn't." He headed for the front door, grabbed his toolbox, then aimed a finger at the back door of the house off the dining room. "Come on. The sooner we get this door secure, the sooner I'll be able to take a deep breath and know you're safe."

Trey made quick work of screwing the pieces of the door frame together to secure it until Macey could have a new door installed. He also braced boards across the door to prevent it from being shoved open since the lock had been splintered.

While he cleaned up his mess, Macey prowled the house, conducting a second inspection of the rooms to determine which was the worst. The first time through, with Trey and the police, she'd been focused on big-ticket items that might be missing. This time, her eyes took in the carnage of dumped drawers and ransacked closets.

Trey joined her at the door to Olivia's old room, which until tonight had remained largely untouched. With no close family to claim her stuff and her aunt living in California and unable to pack up the personal belongings, Macey had left it alone, unwilling to erase her best friend's existence from the planet so quickly.

Now everything had been destroyed. The mattress had been cut with something sharp and foam littered the floor. "I don't understand any of this."

Even Kito seemed to be done with the intrusion to their life. He dropped to the floor outside the bedroom door with a heavy thud.

Trey's hand found the small of Macey's back and rubbed tiny circles there as though he thought it would comfort her. She stepped into the room, pulling away from his touch.

He didn't follow. "What don't you understand?"

She shrugged. "Why this kind of destruction? I mean, my electronics are still sitting where I left them. None of my money is missing. It's like they were…

Like they were looking for something specific. And the worst of the mess is in here. In Olivia's room. But they didn't take anything. Her jewelry box is still there." She walked over to the dresser and picked the box up from where it had been tossed onto the floor. After centering it upright in front of the mirror, she set the picture of her and Olivia on vacation in Denver up beside it. She reached for the second photo that usually sat on the other side of the box, the one Olivia had always guarded closely to her heart.

Only it wasn't there. Macey turned and scanned the room, ignoring Trey's questions, her heart beating faster.

Those men *had* taken something.

And that *something* made no sense whatsoever.

"Find the picture, Trey!" In front of him, Macey became a frantic tornado of rapidly unraveling emotions. She searched through piles of clothing, ducked to look under the bed and then leaned forward to look behind the dresser. "Find it!"

Something weird was going on here. Macey had been a study in calm denial for hours and now a photograph set her off? Had her wall of denial—or guilt—finally cracked? "Macey." Trey gently grabbed her by the shoulders and slowly turned her to face him, half-afraid she'd fight the way Gia had when she'd— When he'd caught her in her dissolving web of lies.

But Macey wasn't Gia. Her distress was genuine. She was upset, not angry.

Trey squeezed her shoulders. "What's going on? What picture?"

She shook her head, still scanning the room as though the photo she was searching for might materialize out of thin air if she simply kept looking for it. It definitely seemed her emotions had finally overtaken her reason; that the reality of the break-in had finally…well, broken through.

Gently, Trey grasped her chin and stilled her frantic searching. He lowered his voice and tried to make her look him in the eye, to ground her into something real so she wouldn't fly apart. "Look at me, Mace. Right here. In front of you. Everything's okay. I promise." The biggest lie he'd ever told. He was the guy who might wind up proving she needed to be put away behind maximum security bars for the rest of her life. He definitely wasn't the one who should be trying to reassure her that her life was okay right now.

But it was all part of the game.

With a suddenness that jarred him, her brown eyes latched on to his and she froze.

So did he.

This was the closest he'd ever been to her, face-to-face. The longest they'd ever made eye contact. Where he'd expected to find calculated cunning and manipulation, he saw instead vulnerability and…fear. The last two things he'd half wished for but had never truly expected.

The purity of her expression rocked him to the core. He'd looked bad guys in the eye before. Had watched more than one man and woman try to manipulate the system. Had even seen his own wife try to fake her way out of her lies. But never had he seen anyone do it so successfully, with such utter guileless innocence behind their eyes.

Macey was scared. And something was wrong. So very wrong. This was not the behavior or the expression of a woman riddled with guilt or hiding something. This was—

He broke eye contact and pulled away, his heart tugging toward her in a way it definitely could not. His eyes could deceive him. His emotions could betray him. No matter what the commander had cautioned him about guilt and innocence, Macey was very likely—no, almost definitely—a criminal. He was investigating her. There was no room for pity or real friendship or more.

And there was definitely no room for whatever had stirred inside his chest. Something he hadn't felt since long before his marriage imploded on a mountain of collapsing lies and betrayal.

He closed his eyes and stepped away from Macey, releasing her. People lied. Even people he'd believed to be the most trustworthy in the world. His ex had sure proved that with her double life. There was no reason Macey had to be innocent just because she had beautiful brown eyes.

No reason at all.

He shook off the feelings and found his rational self somewhere behind his foolish heart. "Okay. Picture." Why did his voice shake? *Seriously?* He cleared his throat. "What's this picture we're looking for? Why's it so important?"

Macey sank against the dresser and crossed her arms. It wasn't a defensive move. It looked more like the posture of a woman trying to hold herself together.

Stay focused, Blackburn. Don't trust vibes. Don't trust your gut. Trust the evidence.

"Olivia had a boyfriend. He traveled a lot for work and they ran in some of the same circles. She met him on one of her business trips. I think he's the reason she kept volunteering to travel, even though she hated it."

"Wait. Olivia was dating someone?" How had he missed that? And could he be the man they'd suspected Olivia was meeting but had never captured on surveillance?

Macey's eyes glazed with something Trey couldn't read. "He died in a private plane crash about a month before you moved in next door."

So Olivia died in a car wreck overseas and her boyfriend had fallen victim to an accident, as well? If those two similar deaths were coincidence, Trey would give up watching hockey for the rest of his life.

He fought to keep his posture neutral. The things Macey was saying lined up with their evidence, with Olivia's guilt…and, unfortunately, with Macey's, as well. "Olivia traveled a lot. Do you remember where?"

Macey shrugged. "You know she was an intelligence contractor, so I really didn't get to be privy to a lot she did or a lot of places she went. All of that top secret security clearance stuff. They don't exactly hand those things out to physical therapists, you know?"

"I know." He refrained from saying too much, even though he wanted to shotgun blast questions at her. The less he said, the more she'd talk. Experience had unfortunately taught him that, as well.

"Anyway, she only had one picture of herself with him, one print she kept beside her jewelry box. Said it wouldn't be good to have pics floating around in the cloud somewhere just because of..." She flittered her hand through the air like a butterfly. "Because of whatever reason she's always been so crazy about online privacy and security and all of that stuff."

What Trey wouldn't give to get his hands on that picture. It might simply be a photo of a woman and her boyfriend, or it might be the key that unlocked this entire investigation.

With a photo, they could put all of the pieces into place. Surely. Maybe they could even clear Macey. He tried his best not to fist his hands. "You're sure it's missing?"

"I don't see it. We can look for it as we clean up. But I guess it's really not important now that Olivia's gone. The fact that something precious only to her is missing makes me feel extra violated. Like this is personal somehow. It's weird those guys would take something so random."

Not so weird if that was the thing they were searching for, if they'd somehow found out there was photographic evidence linking buyer and seller. Maybe that was exactly why they'd hit this house. Why Macey's room hadn't been touched. They'd found what they'd come for.

Or maybe the photo was still here.

He bent and picked up a pair of athletic socks, then dropped them in a drawer. Maybe Macey would follow his lead and they'd find the photo buried under some of the mess left behind.

She did, gathering T-shirts, remarking that she should really donate them now that Olivia's room had been disturbed. By the time they'd finished putting everything away and cleaning the mess from the mattress, nearly an hour had passed and there was no photo.

Maybe he could get a description. It was better than nothing. "You ever meet the guy?"

"What guy?" Macey shoved a drawer shut and wiped her hand at invisible dust on the dresser.

"Olivia's guy." He sat on the edge of the ruined bed and watched her fuss with some smaller items.

"Yeah, on one of her business trips to Denver. She had a ton of frequent-flier miles and took leave for a few extra days. She took me with her. That's the kind of friend she was. I'd never have been able to afford that kind of trip on my own. The hotel alone was…" She shot him a look over her shoulder, one that was half teasing and half confused. "Why do you want to know?"

Trey shrugged one shoulder. "I never saw her date anybody. In all of the times we hung out together, I never heard her mention anyone. Call it curiosity about what kind of guy would catch Olivia's eye."

"She grieved Jeff's death pretty hard. I'm not surprised you never saw her with anyone after him." She hip-checked a drawer shut and headed past him into the living area of the house. "You upset she never looked twice at you?"

"Uh, no. Olivia was too…" He let the word trail off. Probably he shouldn't go insulting Macey's best friend if he wanted to stay on her good side.

"Paranoid? Obsessive? Controlling?" Macey pulled a laptop out of a cabinet under the television and carried it to the counter that divided the den from the living room. She opened the device and ran her fingers along the trackpad to wake it up. "You wouldn't be saying anything I didn't know. Olivia was definitely one of a kind. And she could be tough to live with, that's for sure. But she was…" She stared at the closed blinds over the back window.

"A good friend?"

"Yeah. And that's why I went against her wishes and made a scan of the photo and stored it on the hard drive of the computer she used to run the security system. If she ever lost it for some reason, I wanted her to have a copy. That laptop doesn't have connectivity, so I figured her overly cautious self couldn't object too much if she ever found out."

Macey punched a few keys. "It was taken when we went out to dinner on the last night of our trip to Denver. I was the fourth, sort of the company for Jeff's brother to keep the guy from feeling like a third wheel. Or maybe he was there to keep *me* from feeling like one. I'm not sure." She turned the screen toward him.

Trey nearly lost his balance and grabbed the back of a bar stool. Smiling back at him were Olivia and Macey seated at a table with Jeffrey and Adrian Frye, the very men Eagle Overwatch was trying to take down.

FOUR

Trey tried again to get comfortable on the leather sofa, turning onto his side and wedging his pillow tighter under his head. How could a couch that sat so comfortably for ball games be an absolute beast to sleep on?

Okay, so maybe the couch was more comfortable than his brain and body wanted to admit. And maybe it wasn't the thing robbing him of sleep.

The absolutely senseless puzzle laid out before him had tangled his thoughts and fired his brain up to eleven.

Literally nothing about this night or Macey or their case made any sense at all. The more he learned, the less he knew.

Either she was a master criminal the likes of which his team had never seen, or she was completely innocent of everything the evidence seemed to say she was guilty of. Her bewilderment and wrung-out emotions tonight had seemed very real. Then there was the fact that she'd literally handed him the missing piece of evidence that linked her to two heinous criminals. Was that photo a ploy to make him think she wasn't involved? Or was she truly an innocent bystander to someone else's horrible, deadly game?

He reached for his phone and pulled up the photo he'd surreptitiously snapped of Macey's computer screen earlier, hoping the image would have changed. Nope. Still the two men who called themselves Jeffrey and Adrian Frye, real names unknown. Still suspected of being the masterminds behind countless computer hacks around the country, hacks that had disrupted everything from local hospitals to city power grids. While they were most closely linked to an organization known as Sapphire Skull, the two seemed to glory in being guns for hire, doing the work of anyone who wanted to wreak havoc, claiming the name of whoever paid them the highest price at the moment.

More than once, they'd seemed to act on intelligence they could only have received from someone on the inside of the US intelligence community. Someone like Olivia.

Only Olivia was dead, and the stolen intel still flowed unchecked.

There should be a burning passion inside him to bring Macey to justice, a disgust with her seemingly criminal behavior. It sure was there for the Frye brothers.

Yet, for Macey, he could only battle a sick feeling in his gut that something was wrong. That she was innocent.

He desperately needed to talk this new intel out with Captain Harrison, but he had to be careful. Their texts weren't secure, so he couldn't reach out that way. He could call from Olivia's room, located on the other side of the house from Macey's, but if Macey got up and overheard him, then the whole operation was blown.

A quick glance at his watch told him it was the darker side of three in the morning. Maybe he could slip out and head home for a few minutes, pass along the intel, then come back.

Except Macey had set the alarm and he had no idea what the code was. He was stuck inside. Trapped.

The idea of not being able to get out ran heat across his skin. Only one other time had he been stuck in a place he couldn't get out of, and it had been Gavin Harrison who'd shown up in his hospital room and pulled him out of a pit. Still, the memory congealed in his stomach, disturbing the churning that Macey had already stirred.

He laid his phone next to his pistol on the coffee table and flipped onto his back again, resigned to counting the minutes until sunrise. There was no telling what time—

A soft thud sounded from the deck at the back of the house.

Trey froze.

It could be an animal. Their proximity to the woods wouldn't rule out a stray critter, although with Kito's scent all over the yard, it wasn't likely many animals would be that brave. He tensed, waiting to see if Kito would react from behind the closed door to Macey's bedroom. Not likely, since huskies never barked and were notoriously bad guard dogs, but there was always a chance.

Aside from the music she'd turned on as white noise

shortly after disappearing to catch some sleep, silence reigned inside the house.

Silence reigned outside, too. He eased against the sofa cushions but kept his eye on the back door, somewhat visible in the dim light that filtered into the house from outside. If anyone breached an entrance, the alarm would let the whole neighborhood know, but he couldn't relax. The back of his neck tingled, something that rarely happened when all was well.

Another series of thuds sent Trey's hand for his gun on the coffee table. Those weren't random noises.

Those were footsteps. Someone was outside. Someone who clearly knew the back door had been compromised earlier and was back to try again.

A heavy object collided with the door and a muffled curse followed the blow.

Nice. That someone outside hadn't counted on Trey, a drill and some heavy-duty, two-by-four reinforcement.

He almost smiled as he fired off a quick text to the detective he'd befriended after the initial break-in, then crept to the back door. Trey pressed his back to the wall beside it and waited to see what the nighttime visitor would do with his chosen point of entry sealed.

Of course, Trey was stuck, as well. While he wanted to apprehend this guy dead to rights on Macey's deck, his repair job on the door not only walled him out but walled Trey in. With the alarm on and his need to keep Macey in the dark about the investigation for as long as possible, he'd have to wait until the visitor found another way in or the police arrived.

At least he knew Macey was safe in her room. Her

window was too high off the ground and not accessible from the deck, so he could wait.

His phone vibrated.

Patrol in the neighborhood. Advised them to swing by. No lights or sirens.

He slipped his phone into his hip pocket with a nod. Trey had explained the bare bones of the situation to Detective Franklin, but the man had promised discretion. The last thing he needed was for Macey to figure out she was being investigated and had now been targeted by an unknown assailant. If she was guilty, she might go on the run. If she was innocent, she'd be terrified.

A familiar soft scrape came from Olivia's room down a short hallway on the other side of the dining room.

Trey's grip on his pistol tightened. Someone had opened a window and was likely entering the house.

In silence. The alarm hadn't sounded.

Slipping quietly across the dining room, Trey crept past the linen closet and up the short hall until he reached the doorway to Olivia's room.

A dark figure slid through the window and straightened.

Trey raised his pistol and aimed at center mass. "Most people ring the doorbell." He kept his voice low, hoping neither Macey nor Kito would hear. Not that Kito had ever barked at anything.

The figure froze, a silent shadowed statue in the moonlight.

Steeling himself for a fight, Trey steadied his weapon.

The intruder dived through the low window, cracking his head on the casing and scrambling up to run as soon as he hit the deck.

Trey rolled his eyes and made a quick check of the area for an accomplice before he climbed out the window and raced down the deck stairs, following the mystery intruder to the front of the house. The man vaulted the fence, with Trey not far behind, and they raced toward the subdivision's main road. As a police cruiser came into sight, the guy turned and ran between two houses, angling for the woods and the street on the other side.

Headlights swept up from behind Trey and across the front of his house as the police cruiser rolled to a stop.

Backup. Exactly what he needed.

"Police! Stop and lift your hands!"

Trey skidded to a halt as his suspect disappeared. He was the only one in sight. They were talking to him, because he was running from the house.

And he was carrying a gun.

Macey flopped onto her back and stared at the ceiling as the morning sun strong-armed its way through her thin plastic blinds.

She groaned. Last night, she'd dropped into bed so completely worn-out that she hadn't closed the blackout curtains. Now, at dawn, she was paying the price.

Rolling over, she slapped the off button on the wireless speaker that had pumped instrumental music into her room all night long. She always slept with silence, but her mind had been way too in tune with every single settling pop and creak in the house. Music had been the only antidote to her straining ears. It had worked, too. Aside from hearing Trey moving around sometime after three, nothing had interrupted her sleep.

Something cool and wet nudged her wrist before a furry head slipped under her fingers. Kito. Rolling onto her side, she took the dog's face in her hands and rested her forehead against his. "Always angling for attention, aren't you?"

Excited as only a husky could be, Kito bucked his head, cracking his skull against hers and almost toppling her head backward. "Nice, dude." Rubbing her forehead, Macey sat up, wrinkled her forehead and then nodded as a familiar scent wafted in from the kitchen. Bacon.

That was what had Kito so excited.

The scent of wood-smoked bacon and fresh coffee seemed to fill the room. That dog did love his bacon. Apparently, so did her neighbor.

Guess he'd decided to stay the morning, too.

Tugging a sweatshirt over her head and socks onto her feet, Macey padded to the door and up the short hallway, then peeked around the corner.

Trey stood in the kitchen at the stove, his back to her. He was already dressed and clearly ready for the day, wearing jeans and a navy blue sweatshirt. Even from the back, though, she could tell his hair was tousled from what little sleep he'd probably gotten on her couch.

It was weird, having him in her kitchen this early in the morning. Sure, he'd spent hours and hours hanging out with her and Olivia and, lately, just her, but breakfast had never been involved. It was different.

It shouldn't make her stomach all warm and fuzzy. Probably she was just hungry. And, well, bacon.

Kito had had enough waiting. He squeezed his fifty-seven-pound body between her and the door frame, bolting for the kitchen and drawing Trey's attention from the stove.

"'Bout time you got up." Trey jerked a thumb over his shoulder at the back door. "I took the boards down so you could let Kito out when you got up, but I couldn't open it because of the alarm."

A strange look accompanied his statement before he turned back to the stove. Maybe he thought this whole breakfast thing was a little weird, too.

She walked into the kitchen to the keypad by the garage door and punched in the code. "Is that why you're cooking breakfast? Because you were trapped in the house?"

"A man's got to eat. It's after nine, so I went digging in your fridge. Hope that's okay."

"It's what time?" A glance at the clock on the stove's display confirmed he was telling the truth. She hardly remembered falling asleep, yet it had apparently been over six hours. "Wow."

After she let Kito into the backyard for his morning run, she dropped onto a bar stool and watched Trey work. "I don't usually eat breakfast."

"So the bacon is for…?"

"BLTs. Or I was going to wrap it around those little sausages and put them in the slow cooker with some brown sugar and stuff and have them for the next hockey game." Trey liked those. She'd watched him almost single-handedly clear a plate of them once. How he stayed in shape was beyond her.

Not that she cared what shape he was in. Other than he was her friend and, you know, she wanted all of her friends to be healthy.

She should really stop thinking now.

"In that case, I'll be bringing you more bacon as soon as I can get to the store." He slid a plate across the bar to her and handed over a fork. "Eat up. We have to make a run to the home improvement store so you can get a whole new door frame and I can put it in today. I don't like the idea of boards being the only thing between you and the outside world. I think I'll buy you some new locks, too. Dead bolts that sink a little deeper into the frame to make it harder to kick the door in."

Macey stopped, her fork loaded with eggs halfway to her mouth. "For you to be so certain this was a one-time random act, you sure are acting like you're worried those guys will come back." She lowered the fork to the plate as creeping dread settled like a rock in her stomach and robbed her of her appetite. "You talked to the detective outside for a long time last night. Do you know something I don't?"

"I know you'd better eat and get moving if you want a door installed today. I have to go in for a meeting later this afternoon and I'd really like to not leave a gaping hole in your house for the gnats and mosquitoes to find." He aimed his finger at her plate. "Chow down."

"Seriously, Trey. This is my safety we're talking about. I think I deserve to know everything you do."

He eyed her for a moment, then leaned back against

the island and crossed his arms, staring at her plate. "I'm worried about your alarm."

Her alarm? "It's fine."

"It didn't go off when those guys busted in."

"Like you said last night, maybe I just got distracted and missed a key or something." Although that had never happened before, there was always a first time. "Kito was kind of wound up last night anyway. Maybe you're right and I wasn't paying attention."

His gaze drifted over her shoulder to the back door and then to something above her head. His eyes never met hers.

"Trey…"

"You armed the doors and the windows last night before you went to bed?"

"Yes."

With a heavy breath, he finally met her gaze and held on. "When I took the boards off the back door this morning, it popped open. Not a peep from the alarm. You're sure you—"

"Before I turned it off just now, it said it was armed. You heard the three beeps when I disarmed it. That only happens when it's been turned on and I turn it off." She swallowed hard against a wave of fear, then shook her head. "Maybe back when I reset it after Olivia died, I messed something up. I'm sure that's it. I may have accidentally turned it off. I'm not tech savvy like she was. And how would I ever know I'd messed something up if I never set it off?"

Trey nodded slowly. "I'm sure that's it."

That had to be it. She'd made a mistake.

Anything else would mean the break-in was aimed at her for some reason, and that was a nightmare she never wanted to imagine.

FIVE

In all of the months he'd been watching Macey and Olivia, he'd never been as vigilant as he was in the home improvement store. Although the cavernous building was practically empty of shoppers on a weekday mid-morning, potential danger lurked everywhere. The parking lot could be hiding someone waiting to run her down with their vehicle. The high shelves held heavy equipment and supplies that could easily be shoved down onto Macey's head.

Not that the previous night had given him any chance to sleep and even have a nightmare. It had taken a phone call to the detective and some serious discussion to convince the officers on the scene that he was the good guy. They'd finally set off into the woods after the suspect, but by then he'd been long gone.

Trey had collected a sample of the blood the bad guy had left on the window when he'd fled, cleaned up and set everything back to rights without Macey ever being the wiser. How she'd slept through all of the commotion, he'd never know. If he hadn't been there…

He shuddered and inched closer to Macey's back as

she led the way to the rear of the store, where the exterior doors were kept. When she stopped dead in the middle of the lighting aisle, he crashed right into her and had to scramble backward to keep from tumbling them both to the concrete floor.

She turned on him. "What is your problem today? You're like my baby cousin when we were kids and he'd walk right on my heels to try to see if he could step on the backs of my shoes so I'd walk out of them." She shook her head. "Boys."

Trey had met her "baby" cousin once. He was a six-foot-three army ranger who made even Trey feel like a scrawny weakling. "Just not paying attention. Didn't sleep well last night. Sorry."

She pursed her lips, considered him for a moment, then turned and started walking again. "You act like I need a bodyguard. Nobody's after me. I'm perfectly safe." Reaching back, she grabbed his arm and tugged him forward to walk beside her. "Unless, like I said before, you know something I don't."

Even though she'd let go of his arm as quickly as she'd grabbed it, the heat of her touch still burned on his skin through his sweatshirt. To be honest, half of his distraction was because of her. The more the evidence stacked up against her, the more she seemed completely oblivious. And the more Trey solidified the belief that she was innocent.

And the more he wondered if she was innocent, the more he felt this strange tug toward her.

Or maybe it was the other way around. He felt the tug and that made him want to believe she was innocent.

Whatever was influencing what, it was trashing his

investigative thoughts and messing with his deductive reasoning skills. He couldn't be attracted to her. She was a suspect. He was an undercover investigator who had a lot to prove even still.

Falling for a suspect was a rookie mistake. One he hadn't even made as a rookie.

Then again, he'd never been close friends with a female before, at least not since elementary school. He'd skipped friendship with Gia and gone straight to dating.

It was probably natural to feel a little tug deeper into the friendship.

Whoa. No. Macey wasn't his friend. For a brief few moments he'd forgotten even that. What was wrong with him? If this kept up, he'd have to fess up to the commander and walk away from the investigation.

That would be career suicide.

Fingers wrapped into the back of his shirt and jerked him backward. "Trey. We're at the doors. You're still walking."

He stopped and turned to face the aisle full of exterior doors. "Sorry. Tired."

"So you've said." Macey marched up the aisle and stopped at a door with double-paned glass windows in the top half. "This one. Find a salesman and let's go."

Trey shook himself out of his funk and ran his hand down the door. It was metal and heavy, as solid as solid got. The glass was reinforced and thick enough to withstand some serious force before it shattered. The tag indicated it was meant to discourage break-ins. "You chose that one pretty quickly."

"I've had my eye on it for a while but never had a reason to buy it. That back door's isolated from street view. I figured if I ever had the money, I'd buy one that no one could kick in. Could never justify the expense. But now that it's happened…" She shrugged and stared at the door. "Well, now I have no reason not to."

All morning she'd seemed completely oblivious to what she had to realize: someone was after her specifically, likely because of what she knew. Or who she knew. But the entire thing seemed to confuse her.

Then, just when she seemed innocent, she did something like research industrial-strength doors. The kinds of doors that said someone was hiding something.

Yeah, he really did need to have a long talk with Captain Harrison.

Macey shoved him in the biceps. "Go find someone to write this up and then we can go home. If you get done in time, I can go into the office and catch up on some medical files. Even if I have the day off, I'm behind, and I'm antsy to keep moving so I don't start thinking again."

There was no arguing with Macey when she had a goal in mind. Trey had learned that the hard way over the past year or so. With a quick, flippant salute, he marched down the aisle in search of help. Leaving Macey wasn't his favorite idea, but she was already suspicious of him. It wasn't like something would happen in the thirty seconds he was away from her. If she was going to run, she'd have done it during the night while she'd believed he was asleep. And if someone was going to come after her, they'd pick a much less public place to attack. They'd proved that with the second attempted entry into the house last night.

It took a little bit longer than he wanted to find an

associate, and by the time he made it back to the aisle where he'd left Macey, his mind had spun up a thousand different ways she could have died while he was absent. He rounded the corner with his brain primed to feel relief when he spotted her, but the aisle was empty.

Macey was gone.

Macey ran her finger down a shower door, then stepped back to look at the display. Trey would be back soon and would wonder where she'd wandered off to, but she needed a second. He was crowding her with staying at the house last night and just now dogging her footsteps like a sheepdog trying to herd her through the aisles. It was hard to breathe.

Honestly, she needed some time to process the break-in without adding Trey's odd behavior to it. He'd been a great neighbor and a good friend ever since he'd rented the house next door, someone she trusted completely, but last night's events seemed to have set him on high alert. Maybe his house had been invaded when he was a kid. Maybe it had something to do with his work on post.

Maybe he was just way more overprotective than she'd ever imagined.

Macey jerked open the door to another shower display and stuck her head inside. Her bathroom was way too small. If only she had the money to—

A force from behind shoved her forward, smashing her cheek into the plastic shower wall and bending her neck at an awkward angle. Pain shot down her spine and she tried to scream, but only a whimper escaped from her twisted neck.

Someone leaned hard against her back, their hand against her face, blocking her vision and forcing her head against the wall until she was sure her skull was going to implode. Her mind raced through every self-defense move she knew and came up empty. She tried to fight, tried to struggle, tried to get free, but the attacker's full weight was on her, too heavy to allow her any movement in the small space and too close to allow her any way to counterattack.

Her heart pounded so hard she could see the pulse in her eyes. She was trapped. There was no way out this time.

Warm sweat broke out on her skin and she whimpered, desperate for air. Desperate for help. Desperate, desperate, desperate.

Hot breath hit her ear and Macey's knees weakened as she realized her attacker was a man. If the guy hadn't been pressing her to the wall, she'd have collapsed. Harsh words followed his breath. "Where is it?"

The words hardly computed, could hardly be heard over the roar in her ears. She couldn't breathe. The world was growing dark. If she passed out, what would he do to her?

He leaned impossibly closer, his body weight pressing the air from her lungs. "Tell me or I'll kill you right here."

The man shifted and something sharp stung in a slice along her side through her sweatshirt.

While that terrified her more than his presence, his movement released the pressure of his weight and his hand just enough for her to do something about it.

Macey drove her elbow back into his side and connected solidly with his ribs. He grunted and dropped back farther.

Cool air rushed into the space between them and Macey drew in a deep breath, then tried to scream.

It came out as a terrified squeak, but it was enough. From the next aisle, Trey called her name, his voice frantic.

The man shoved against Macey and fled.

She slid to the floor, her knees hitting with a thud that shot pain throughout her body. Her forehead rested against the cool plastic shower wall as she gasped for air. She was alive. She was okay. The man was gone.

A slight warmth trickled down her side and she slipped her hand under her sweatshirt. Her fingers slid along something warm and wet. Blood? He'd stabbed her?

Outside, Trey called her name again, closer this time. And though she tried to call back, her racing heart choked off her air so that the words just wouldn't come out above a whisper. She pressed her hand to the wall to help herself up, leaving bloody fingerprints behind. Macey stumbled over the lip of the shower and onto all fours in the aisle, shaking.

Every part of her body shaking.

Trey dropped to his knees beside her. "Macey? Mace? Look at me. Look me in the eye."

She turned her head toward the sound of his voice, but the roar in her ears was too loud as the room grew increasingly dark. Blackness crept in from the side and narrowed her vision.

Trey looked over his shoulder at someone. "Call an ambulance."

Grabbing for his arm, Macey tried to force him to look at her. When he turned back to her, she had to push the words out on a breath. "Bleeding…"

But the world faded into a black roar.

SIX

When the door between the ER and the waiting room at Cape Fear Valley Medical Center opened, Trey stood for what had to be the hundredth time.

It was no one he knew.

He'd followed the ambulance to the hospital, and the fifteen-minute ride had felt more like fifteen hours. On arrival, he'd been blocked from seeing Macey. Because he wasn't family and Macey was in no condition to vouch for him, he'd been left to wait. When her mother had arrived, she'd rushed to Macey's side, promising to pass news along to Trey as soon as she had some. Knowing Tiffany Price's flair for excitement, it would be a while. As long as she could soak up sympathy from the doctors and receive attention as the worried mother, she'd stick by her daughter. When the storm was gone, she would be, too.

The small waiting room hummed with low voices. It smelled like a hospital, that unexplainable antiseptic-and-sickness odor that still curdled his stomach, even after all these years. Only that time, it had been his platoon anxiously pacing the waiting room while he lay in surgery.

With a jerk of his shoulders, Trey glanced around the room at the sick and injured who were waiting, some wearing surgical masks and all looking like they'd rather be anywhere but there.

As his heart pounded and his skin broke into a cold sweat, his mind raced out of control. He couldn't take any more. Turning on one heel, he walked out the emergency entrance, past the security guard, and inhaled deep breaths of cool spring air. It might be filled with pollen, but it was fresh.

There was a big difference between his prior situation and Macey's. Even though her mother was a monumental flake, Macey still had family by her side somewhere in the depths of the hospital. And this situation wasn't squarely her fault.

At a brisk pace, he crossed the driveway and dropped onto a bench near the parking attendant's booth, then leaned his head back to stare at the bright Carolina blue sky. He was way too deep in his own head for his own good.

It had him frozen, reacting instead of responding. Worse, reacting instead of grabbing this thing by the throat and taking the lead. Straightening, he pulled out his cell phone and dialed Captain Harrison to give him a situation report and lay out his next step. A step that twisted in his gut as though *he* was the bad guy in this entire scenario.

When the commander answered with his typical normal-guy "Hello?" Trey glanced around to make sure no one was in earshot.

"Blackburn?" Harrison's voice cut in, deep with concern. "Everything good?"

Trey was taking too long to answer, but he honestly wasn't sure what to say or even why he'd called.

The mission. He had to focus on the mission, even if his head was muddy between past and present, between duty and... And how it had felt to see Macey on the concrete floor with a bloodstain spreading across the side of her sweatshirt.

That was the real issue.

"Sorry." He cleared his throat and watched an older gentleman help his wife from a wheelchair into a gray sedan on the other side of the parking lot. "We have a minor situation."

"I'm all ears." There was that business voice, the one that said the commander knew it was bigger than a *minor situation*.

Trey ran down the events of the morning, feeling even more like a dog for leaving Macey alone in the home improvement store. But who would have thought someone would attack her in the open?

"How is she?" His commander needed answers and facts before he'd be ready to talk about anything else.

Like next steps. Awful next steps.

"I haven't had an update since they brought her in, but it's only been about twenty minutes. Her mother met the ambulance here and is with her. She had a fair amount of blood loss, but I've seen a whole lot worse, so my guess is it was a shallow cut. Probably enough for stitches but not enough to do damage. I'll link up with the police contact I have later to see what the official report says, but someone found a box cutter near the scene." He prayed her wound truly was minor. If Macey suffered unduly because of him...

Even if she was one of the bad guys, she deserved justice, not to be cut down in the plumbing aisle of a home improvement store.

"A box cutter would make sense. Easy to grab in the store and it wouldn't look out of place if our guy was carrying it around. We'll get access to surveillance footage. There could be a clue here that blows this whole thing wide-open."

Leaning forward, Trey rested his elbows on his knees. He held the phone tight against his ear with one hand and kneaded the tension in his neck with the other. "Why the sudden activity? What's changed? That's what I don't get. We have all of these pieces that say Macey is involved, but no concrete evidence she ever handed over any intel or took any money. Now, suddenly, someone has escalated to invading her home and direct physical assault? It's not adding up. Especially when all they took from the house was the photo of Frye that was in Olivia's room. Macey's room was untouched. If she was the target..." He exhaled loudly. "I just don't know what to think anymore, sir."

"Where are you?"

Pushing straight again, Trey glanced around to make sure no one had wandered within earshot. "Outside the ER."

Silence stretched long over the phone line. There was a light tapping, as though Harrison had picked up a pencil and was letting the eraser repeatedly hit the table. It was a move Trey had seen often when the man had something on his mind. "When was the last time you were in a hospital? Or even near a hospital?"

Trey didn't need to respond. The captain already knew the answer to that question.

"Blackburn, you're not the same man you used to be. Sooner or later you're going to have to trust that's true."

Trust. Funny word, that one. "I get it. All of that new creation stuff in Corinthians." Captain Harrison had preached it to him time and again. He was different, no longer who he used to be. It was all true. Trey trusted Jesus. The problem was—

"You don't trust yourself."

"And there you go, reading my mind again." Trey shook his head, trying to throw off the memories. A horrible night with horrible consequences that should have ended his miserable life. Except he was still here, the very definition of a second chance.

A second chance with a job to do, even though the next part of his plan made him nauseous. "Listen, back to the job at hand. I have an idea."

"You sound like that idea involves you eating rotted earthworms."

He hadn't meant for his repulsion to show up in his voice. Sometimes, Captain Harrison was too intuitive. It made him the best investigator Trey had ever met, but that same trait made it really hard to work with him.

Trey took a deep breath and charged forward. "There's an issue with Macey's security system. It's either not being armed or these guys have found a way to remotely disarm it." He slowed, thinking. "That would make no sense because it's a closed system. There's no access from the outside." He'd have to look into that. "Anyway.

The system is run by a laptop that is hardwired in when changes need to be made. That laptop has no connectivity. The kicker is, it belonged to Olivia."

"Can you get access to that machine?" The commander's voice pitched up. He smelled the same thing Trey did. The scent of answers. Of a trail that might not be as cold as they'd thought.

"I can get the password from Macey, tell her I want to dig into the system to see if I can figure out what's going on with the alarm. If she says yes, that will give me not only the password but consent to do some searching."

"That makes anything you find there admissible." Something scraped against the phone, and Trey knew the commander was rubbing his cheek, another thinking tic of his. "It will also tell you a lot about her level of guilt, too. If she holds that laptop close, it's a point against her, but if she gives up that password easily..."

Then it might be considered further evidence that she had nothing to hide. That would only leave Trey more uncertain about who Macey was and what game, if any, she was playing.

Every muscle in her body hurt.

Macey shifted on the horribly uncomfortable hospital bed and tried to push up taller to relieve some of the pinching pain in her side, but her mother's hand on her shoulder stopped her.

With a wry smile, her mother pressed the button to raise the head of the bed slightly. "Better?" For the moment, Tiffany Price was the dutiful, attentive mother, but no doubt that would soon pass now that Macey was about to be released.

Macey would take what she could get. "Yeah. But if it hurts this much numbed from them sewing it all back together, how much is it going to hurt later?"

Maybe if she focused on the dozen stitches in her side, she'd forget how the wound got there in the first place. While the cut wasn't life-threatening, it was deep enough to merit stitches and IV antibiotics. And the fact she'd fainted was enough to run her through a battery of tests and to hold her in the ER hooked up to monitors that pumped faster every time she thought about hot breath on her cheek and terrifying weight against her back.

Sure enough, the numbers started to climb.

Her mother stood. "Do you want me to call the doctor?"

Oh, she'd love that, wouldn't she? Creating a little bit of excitement because her daughter wasn't recovering quickly? Provide a little drama to the waiting? It'd be nice if she'd just offer her daughter a hug or even a pat on the head.

Yeah, her mother wouldn't do any of that. It was useless to complain. Macey sighed. "Just find out how it is that the same person who had her house broken into gets mugged in the same twenty-four hours. Then make it stop."

A male voice from the door pinged the heart rate monitor higher, but it wasn't Trey. "Not your day, is it?"

Macey tried to tamp down the disappointment at the sight of a uniformed police officer. She managed to dig her voice up, but not before wondering why Trey wasn't there. "Not at all." She waved the officer in and spent the next ten minutes answering his questions about the attack, fighting to stay calm while recalling details she'd rather forget.

Her mother pulled out her phone and slipped away during the conversation, probably catching up on her messages. Why should she stay and support her daughter?

The police officer wrapped up, handed her a business card and left as quickly as he'd arrived.

Macey laid her head back on the pillow and closed her eyes. Why couldn't they just let her go home? Surely she'd be more comfortable there, right? Less afraid. Less—

"Feeling any better?"

This time, the male voice was definitely familiar. Definitely Trey's. And it definitely flooded her system with something she could only call relief. Safety. The same things she was wishing she could find at home.

Macey eased one eye open and refused to think about all of those things her brain wanted her to think.

In the doorway, Trey stood with his hands shoved into his pockets, looking at her with an uncertainty he'd never shown before, almost as though he didn't belong. Did he not realize he had become her closest friend? That he was as welcome here as her mother? In fact, he was probably more welcome.

Macey could tell him that and ease some of his obvious discomfort, but it was a high possibility that pain meds and emotional overload were making her sappy and weepy. "You gonna stand there and stare at me or do you want to come in?"

He flashed her a smile that looked slightly more normal and stepped into the room. "Your mom said it was okay to come back."

Macey laughed, then winced when her side protested. She dropped the mirth to a chuckle. "Sounds like we're kids and Mom said I could come outside to play."

Dropping to the edge of the chair by her bed, Trey offered another weak grin. "I guess so. Have they said when you can head home?"

"As soon as they're convinced I'm not going to pass out again. They've run all kinds of unnecessary tests, but I don't think they plan to admit me." Oh, how she hoped not. After several hours in this hospital bed, she was done.

Trey sat with his elbows braced on his knees, studying his clasped hands.

Macey eased herself up on her elbows. He actually looked a little pale. "Are you okay? Do you need to trade places with me?"

"Huh?" When he lifted his head, it was to stare at the wall in front of him. "No. I just…" He shrugged. "I just don't like hospitals."

"Yet you're here."

"It's you." He turned slightly and his blue eyes caught hers. "Where else would I be?"

The way her heart jolted at the simple words almost made her gasp. Boy, he'd better not be getting an eyeful of the monitor right now. Surely he hadn't meant that the way it sounded. "I… Thank you." His concern was warmth to her battered body. Someone actually did care. Someone actually looked at her and saw her, not only what she could do for them. The realization brought a prickle behind her eyes, but she blinked it away.

"So." Trey slapped his hands onto his knees and stood, walking over to study the board that held information about her nurses and her status. "Your mom said you got stitches?"

"She talked to you?"

"She's the one who sent me back here." Trey turned to face her. "She cares in her own way."

Trey had known her mother for such a short time. He had no idea what growing up alone while her mother did her own thing was really like.

It was better not to talk about that right now, though. "Yes, I got stitches. A dozen of them. Where they are shouldn't keep me from working, though. It wasn't deep, just in a tough spot to heal. No muscle involvement, so I'm good. Police said it was a box cutter from the store, probably a crime of opportunity. Lucky me."

The look on Trey's face said he knew she was avoiding his comment about her mother, but he seemed to think better of pushing it. "Yeah, it's a little odd you'd get hit twice in two days. Kind of makes you want to hide at home, huh?"

Except her home had been a target already. She pulled the blanket closer to her chin, suddenly chilled. "Honestly, it makes me wonder if anywhere's really safe." She muttered the words, but the way Trey's back and shoulders stiffened, there was no doubt he'd heard.

"Look, I'm willing to bunk on your couch or even in the guest room at your house if it makes you feel better. I mean, for a day or two. Or whatever you need." He still studied the board as if it held all of the answers to life's questions. The hair on the back of his head was rumpled, as though he'd been rubbing his hand over it the way she'd seen him do during hockey games when the Blues were down and time was getting tight.

He was anxious. Tense. Nervous.

Because of her.

Macey didn't even want to analyze what that might mean. He was Trey. Her neighbor. Her friend. The guy who had never made a single romantic overture or even hinted at wanting anything more. There was no sense developing some lopsided crush on him just because he'd been her knight in shining armor twice in two days. Just because he cared. That was silly elementary-school behavior. And besides, she'd seen how relationships worked. She'd seen the way her mother treated hers. Used them until the new wore off and then threw them away.

Well, Macey refused to be discarded. "You don't have to stay at my house. I'll be fine." It was easy to say that in a brightly lit and bustling hospital ER. Probably, when the sun went down and the darkness descended, what little bit of bravado she had left would fade with the dying light.

Still, Trey couldn't put his life on hold for her.

"Let me do something." He finally faced her, but he stared at something just to her right. "I feel like this is my fault. Like I need to make up for it. Like if I hadn't left you alone, then the guy who did this to you wouldn't have had the—"

"Like you knew some freak show was going to mug me in the plumbing department. What are the odds?"

"What makes you think it was a mugging?"

"He asked me 'where is it,' like he wanted my wallet. What else would it be?" A wash of cold fear froze her lungs and raced down her spine. "You don't… I mean… Last night…" Surely not. *Surely. Not.* The two incidents couldn't be related. "I've got nothing anybody would want. Nothing they would look for in my house or would cut me to get. Nothing. You don't think this is about me personally, right?" *Say no. Say I can safely go home because all of this is one big awful coincidence.*

Trey walked over and picked up her hand, twining his fingers through hers. He rested his other hand on top, warm and oddly comforting. "You're okay. You're safe. I mean, what could you possibly have done to make someone come after you?"

Truth brought a fragile measure of peace. He was right. "Unless someone is seriously unhappy with the exercises I made them do in physical therapy, nothing." She pulled her fingers from his grip, the feeling all too electric and all too much something she didn't want to end.

Trey rested his hands on the bed rail. "I've been through PT. There were times…" This time his grin was genuine, but it faded quickly. "Your mom's going to want to come back here, and they're only allowing one visitor at a time right now. Want me to go and check on Kito in case you're here for a while?"

Kito. How could she forget her dog? He'd likely torn the house apart in a frantic need to get outside. "Yeah, he probably needs to go out. We've been gone awhile. You can get my key from Mom. I think she has my things in her purse." Hopefully, she hadn't up and left the hospital already.

"Anything else I can do?"

"You didn't happen to buy that door, did you?" She sure could use some levity about now, some restoration in the balance of their friendship. Something that didn't tilt dangerously toward her wanting him to lean down and kiss her.

Why would she want that?

Pain meds. Surely it was pain meds. Although, she was fairly certain they'd only given her Tylenol.

This time his smile was genuine. "I bought it online, and they're delivering it in a couple of hours. You're a top customer-service priority to them after what happened." He held up a hand to stop her from speaking. "Don't say a word about paying me back. We can deal with that another time. I just want you to have a door tonight, okay?"

She knew better than to argue with that look. "Okay."

"And speaking of doors, your alarm has me concerned."

Her, too. It was odd it hadn't gone off the day before or this morning when Trey opened the door. "Like I said, maybe I deactivated something in the system. I can check later."

"Or I can hang out at your house and take a look while I'm waiting for the door to be delivered. I'm not so bad with computer stuff."

Since she had no idea what she'd done to disable the system in the first place, it couldn't hurt to have somebody else see if they could figure it out. If it made her house more secure, that would be a bonus. "Sure. It's that laptop I pulled out earlier, the one that runs the alarm exclusively. It probably needs to be charged, though."

He nodded once. "Password?"

She winced. Maybe she should have chosen a more grown-up one after Olivia set the first one, but it had been a long-standing running joke between them. "It's from a movie."

"Okay?" Trey's eyebrow arched in what might be amusement. He'd probably already guessed which one.

"Inigo Montoya." She looked him dead in the eye and dared him to laugh.

"I knew it. From *The Princess Bride*? That movie you've made me watch a thousand times?" The tight lines in his face said he was trying not to laugh. "And you spell that how?"

Biting back her own smile, Macey spelled the words Olivia had laughingly created as her password. "And don't forget to capitalize *Inigo* and *Montoya*."

"No numbers? No punctuation marks?"

"Nope. And it's all one word, no space. Olivia was all about the funny on that one. I guess she figured the laptop didn't need to be all that secure since it never left the house."

Trey's forehead creased and he started to say something but then backed toward the door. "I'll go take care of Kito and see if I can fix the alarm. I'm sure your mom's ready to come in again." With a nod, he was gone as quickly as he'd appeared.

Macey listened to the sound of his footsteps fading.

Something was wrong with him, and it went past not liking hospitals.

And something was definitely wrong with her, at the way her heart fell as he walked away.

SEVEN

Shutting the door behind him, Trey surveyed the living room, dining room and kitchen of Macey's house. The back door was still barricaded where he'd reinforced the boards before they'd left. Nothing appeared to have been touched in their absence.

No, today the target hadn't been the house. It had been Macey. A direct assault he should have seen coming.

Kito bounded in from his bed in Macey's room and started talking in typical husky howls and whines. Yep. The dog definitely needed to go out. Trey walked him out the front door and through the gate into the backyard and then went back inside. He shut the front door behind him and locked both locks, then walked into the kitchen to secure the dead bolt to the garage. The longer it took Macey to get in if he wasn't finished investigating by the time she came home, the more time he'd have to look innocent when she arrived.

Look innocent. Was that what Macey was doing? Was she devious enough to set up a scenario in which she looked like the victim? Or was she truly a bystander?

It hurt his head—and his heart—just thinking about it. No matter what the evidence said, he was certain he knew Macey well. Even the rest of his team believed she was likely innocent. It was still a tough line for investigators like them to walk.

He tossed her keys on the dining room table, retrieved the laptop and settled it on the bar that separated the living area from the kitchen. He plugged in the machine, then dropped an external hard drive and his cell phone on the counter beside it.

This was his job. Macey had given him permission to be in her house and on this computer, so why did he feel like the lowest form of pond scum?

Trey inserted his earpiece, then dialed Dana Santiago's number. As soon as Dana arrived later this evening, he'd pass the cloned drive to her so she could dig for anything that might finally prove Macey innocent.

Or guilty.

That right there was the thing that gave him pause and made his conscience threaten to run for cover. Everything in him was convinced she was innocent. And not being fully truthful with her at the hospital had left him feeling like he'd just completed the Darby Queen obstacle course at army ranger school. In the mud. Twice. He really ought to—

"This is Dana. You ready to get to this, Trey?" Dana's voice lit up in his ear. A former US marshal with WitSec, Dana Santiago was a tech rock star and a welcome recent addition to Eagle Overwatch's team as a civilian contractor.

Trey needed to be as all business as she was. "I fig-ure I've got about half an hour. As I was pulling into the driveway, Macey called and said they'd finally re-leased her. It'll take them a little bit to do that and then about half an hour to get here from the hospital, but I'm not willing to take any chances." Because if she caught him, that could be the end of everything.

"Then let's get moving. Rich and I are on the road to you. Should be there in a couple of hours and we can amp this thing up."

"Good." As much as he'd chafed at backup at first, today had convinced him he needed it. "What do I need to do?"

"The software to clone the laptop's hard drive is on the external drive you have. Plug it in, crank up the utility, and it's self-explanatory from there. I'm here if you hit any bumps in the road. Should be simple un-less someone hid some partitions in the drive. You're trained enough to sniff those out."

Trey keyed in the password and followed Dana's di-rections, but one thing still nagged at him. "While this is loading, let me run something by you."

"Fire away."

"Say you're you, all tech geeky and stuff, but you're also incredibly paranoid. So paranoid that your alarm system and the laptop that runs it have zero connectiv-ity to the outside world."

"I'd say I'm hiding something major, but go on."

"But your user password contains no special charac-ters, no capital letters, no nothing." It had bugged him since the amusement at the unusual password had died.

It didn't seem like Olivia's standard operating proce- dure to create a password so easily crackable.

Dana sighed. "Who made the password?"

"Olivia."

"Hmm." The sound of silence hung over the line. There was a muffled conversation, probably with Rich, before she spoke again. "I'd say that's pretty suspicious. Almost like she wanted it to be crackable. From what I've heard of her and seen in your reports, she was best described as—"

"Paranoid."

"Well, yes. She had all of the markers of someone trying to hide something."

She did. And, oddly enough, Macey had none of those characteristics. Once again, nothing made sense.

Trey glanced at the clock on the screen and at the progress of the software. He was running out of time quickly. "I'm going to clone the entire hard drive. Macey has the only user data on the system, but I'm going to guess there's more I can't tap into. This is too simple." The more he saw, the more he became con- vinced that Olivia was the guilty party and, somehow, Macey had been dragged into this maze. Unless Macey thought he was too stupid to figure out her laptop was one of the keys to proving guilt or innocence, she had no idea what she'd handed him.

But she could still be lying. After all, he'd missed it with Gia. Everything had seemed fine in his marriage until it wasn't. And he'd been stunned to learn it hadn't been fine for a very long time.

He dug into the system as far as he could go with Macey's credentials. "Okay, there has to be an admin account somewhere on this machine. Macey only has user credentials. Something tells me Olivia buried an account on here. There are some large files deep in the hard drive, but I can't see what type they are. They date from a couple of years ago to as late as yesterday. Random days and times. You can crack into this, I'm sure."

"If Olivia hid something, I can find it. Never underestimate me."

"Never said I did."

From the direction of the kitchen, the hum of the garage door rising froze Trey's fingers on the keyboard. "Macey's home." The status bar still indicated he needed a few more minutes. "I'm going to disconnect our call. When this is done, I'll run back to the house and lock the external drive in the safe in my closet for you to access when you arrive if I'm not there."

"Be safe, Trey." The screen on his phone went blank as Dana killed the call.

Be safe. Why did that still feel like an indictment instead of a sentiment born out of concern? If nothing else, it was a reminder to keep Macey at arm's length, because even though they all suspected she was innocent, she still might not be what she seemed.

The laptop pinged its completion and Trey ejected the hard drive and shoved it into his back pocket as the kitchen door rattled.

A key in the lock and a twist of the knob, and then Macey's mother stepped inside. She glanced at Trey. "Oh good. You're here." She dropped the keys by the stove. "I can head on out, then. She'll be safe with you."

"Where's Macey?"

"She went around to the side of the house to open

the gate and let Kito in." With a wave, Tiffany Price walked out, leaving the door to the garage open.

Trey's stomach clinched. After the events of the past couple of days, the idea of Macey out of his sight, even in her own yard, set his senses on high alert. It shouldn't be that way. It should never be that way. Not for him and not for her, either.

He was half a second from bolting into the yard to make sure she was safe when Kito pounded up the garage steps and skidded on the kitchen tile, headed straight for his water bowl. He lapped with a ferocity that would normally make Trey laugh.

But where was Macey?

Trey took two steps toward the door just as Macey appeared, pale and tired, but upright and safe.

He thought his knees were going to give out and drop him to the floor. Oh man, he was definitely in trouble.

She shut the garage door and leaned back against it. "I saw Mom leave."

Wincing, Trey forced himself not to go to her and hug the look of dejection away. He failed to understand a mother who had no maternal instincts. His own had prayed him through the roughest times of his life, even when he hadn't wanted her to. "She said she'd check on you later."

"You and I both know she didn't say that." Macey tipped her head toward the laptop. "Did you figure it out? Did I completely wreck the system?" She leaned heavily on the counter, appearing tired but none the worse for wear, although she favored her left side a little.

Trey couldn't look at her. While he wasn't about

to lie, he certainly wasn't about to tell her everything he'd been doing in her house while she was absent. He turned his focus to the laptop and clicked on what must be the program that ran the alarm system. "Just now cranking up the alarm software. Would you happen to know if Olivia had a separate account and password?"

"No." Macey walked over to stand beside him, heightening the sense of guilt in Trey's gut. "I guess because I'm computer illiterate, she thought it was funny to make the account in my name. We never used that computer unless it was to control the alarm. After she died, I hid it away so nobody else could get to the alarm system. I guess her paranoia rubbed off on me."

"She had another laptop, then?"

"She had her main laptop with her overseas, and I assume it went to her aunt with the rest of the things she had with her at the time."

Trey shifted to one side so that Macey's arm wouldn't brush his as she looked over his shoulder. The longer this op went on, the more uncomfortable he grew with seeking Macey's guilt. But as the commander had reminded him, he was also searching for her innocence. He simply couldn't let his mind make a decision. He had to stay balanced. So why did he keep swaying toward her?

He steeled himself against her presence and clicked through the alarm system. It was a basic interface with toggle switches for each segment of the alarm. Just as Macey had said, the alarms for the doors and windows were on, while the floor pads and motion sensors were off. It was odd that Olivia had designed something so simple, although she could have simply created a basic user interface for Macey's sake.

Or…

"You said this laptop has no connectivity?"

"None. When I changed the settings, I had to wire it into the main router in the office."

Trey nodded once, then scrolled to the system settings on the machine. He hesitated with the mouse over the program he wanted. It wouldn't be a good thing if she caught sight of the screen and asked exactly what he was doing. "How about you climb into the recliner and get some rest? I'll be done here in a minute and be out of your way until the door is delivered."

"The recliner." Her voice held no small amount of longing. "That sounds amazing."

Trey moved to the small dining room table and sat with his back to the wall, facing the den, where Macey reclined. He clicked into the settings and headed for the network, scrolling through several screens until he confirmed his suspicions. He needed Dana Santiago more than ever, because Olivia had laid out the drive in a way that wouldn't allow it to be fully cloned. And it certainly wouldn't allow Dana to see all that he was seeing. Something that curled his stomach over on itself.

A hidden network interface card was installed on the laptop, one Macey would never have thought to look for. Despite what she believed, the laptop was wirelessly connected to their network.

And someone else was in control of the alarm.

Macey lay on the recliner, half listening to an old sitcom on TV and half watching Trey fiddle with the laptop. He was intent on what he was doing, but he was still there with her. Unlike her mother. No drama, no mama.

Macey sighed. It had always been that way. And it was the exact reason she had to shut down this little crush on Trey. If her own mother couldn't be there for her, why would anyone else? As much as it pained her, even Trey couldn't be fully trusted to be there for her in the end, to truly care when she needed it. One day, even he would vanish.

While Trey was trying to look like he wasn't doing much more than messing with the operating program for the alarm, she'd known him long enough to recognize the furrow in his brow. Something else was going on here. Something she couldn't quite put her finger on. The break-in yesterday and the man at the store today were beginning to tangle together in her emotions and her memories.

Medication had dulled the pain in her side to a consistent, annoying throb. The cut hadn't been deep enough to keep her from working the next day, but it was enough to curb some of her activities for a little while, at least preventing her from doing anything that would pull at her stitches. The doctor had said it was a good thing the man had chosen a box cutter and not something bigger. Probably, in the morning, it wouldn't feel like a good thing.

After much testing and consultation, the doctors had decided her fainting had been nothing more than emotional shock and that her neck and head were fine. But that didn't make any of this feel real. The whole event made everything seem like it was happening to someone else, as though she'd somehow stepped into a movie role and no one had given her a script.

And then there was Trey. He'd always been one of those confident, take-charge kind of guys, almost to the point of being overbearing a few times. Olivia had called him on it more than once. While Macey had noticed it, she'd let the two of them with their competing controlling personalities tough it out with each other. It had been fun to watch them try to get the upper hand, whether in a pickup basketball game or in the decision of where to order pizza for dinner. Usually, if Macey waited long enough, the two of them wore themselves out baiting each other and she was able to step in and win without even trying.

But today, Trey was different. Hesitant at the hospital and uncharacteristically reserved now, he almost seemed like a stranger, a man pulling away from being her friend. Maybe he was about to back out on her, too, just like her mother.

She closed her eyes and winced. That would hurt more than she wanted to admit. This was foolishness. She was violating her own rules about romance and relationships. Trey was her friend and that was all she ever wanted him to be. Anything else was too risky.

"You okay?" Trey's voice came in a soft whisper from the kitchen table.

Opening her eyes, Macey eased herself upright with a pain-driven wince and stood. She walked over and sat across from him. When she did, he pulled the laptop closer and angled the screen even more toward him.

"What are you doing over there? Streaming episodes

of *Gilmore Girls* and you don't want me to know you get all weepy about the goings-on in Stars Hollow?"

With a groan, Trey rolled his eyes. "You know I'm not."

"Sure I do." When they'd fallen into a show hole once on a rare North Carolina snow day, Olivia had won the remote war and had forced Trey to watch the series about a mother and daughter who'd formed a unique and loving friendship. His mutters and the way he'd frequently shoved his face into a pillow said it was too girlie for him, but Macey had caught him watching more than once, and he'd shushed her during a pivotal scene. "I'm guessing if I went over to your house and checked your watch history, you'd be up to season four? Because you know you didn't stop when you left here that day. You were hooked."

"Pleading the fifth." With a last glance at the laptop screen, he moved to close it.

But Macey reached out and pivoted the machine toward her before he could. When Trey made a grab for it, she pulled it from the table into her lap, then made a face at him. "You really are streaming sappy TV shows over here, aren't you?" The laughter died quickly when she caught a glimpse of the screen, though. Instead of the alarm program she'd expected to see, the screen was black and filled with white letters and numbers. "What is this? Why are you this deep into the system?"

When she glanced up at Trey, his face was an emotionless mask. In an instant, though, the passivity was gone, replaced with his normal teasing expression. "I thought you were a computer nobody. How do you know so much about them now?"

"I learned to code a little bit during a summer camp in middle school. This isn't the alarm."

"It sort of is." With a heavy exhalation, he rounded the table and sat in the chair beside hers, gently removing the laptop from her lap to set it between them on the polished hardwood. He swiped the trackpad and, with a click, reopened the user interface for the alarm. He pointed at the screen. "You did everything right. Here, here and here." His finger followed his words, indicating the switches she'd toggled off or on based on the features she'd wanted to keep active.

Macey said nothing. After the past couple of days, she didn't know what to think about Trey's attitude or his actions.

"The bottom line is, the alarm should be working. Based on what I see here, in Olivia's program, there's no reason the door intrusion or the window intrusion shouldn't have set it off."

"Okay. So why—" Macey's head snapped up, pulling at her sore neck muscles. "Window intrusion?" Nobody had come through the window. "The back door was kicked in. Right? Did I miss something?"

Trey shot her a strange look. "*A* window intrusion. A theoretical window intrusion. If someone had opened a window while the alarm was set, it would have gone off based on what you've turned on here." He cleared his throat. "The problem is that when the door was kicked in and when I opened it this morning, it didn't sound. Are you sure Olivia didn't have a separate account set up?"

"I— No." The abrupt question spun her thoughts before she could ground them back into the conversation.

"Is that what you were doing? Trying to hack the system?" *Hack.* After a robbery and a mugging, the word sounded evil and not like Trey at all. Was she growing suspicious of everyone, even the people she knew best?

"Actually, I was trying to look at the system to see if your alarm user interface was actually active. It's possible Olivia made you a simplistic version, an easier one to use, and that she had a more technical system set up under another account. I was looking to see if there was a way to tell. If she did, there could be a glitch between your user interface and the secondary account."

Macey nodded once. It made sense. Trey knew way more about computers than she ever would. While her friends had all been taking tech classes in college, she'd been deep in courses about human anatomy and physiology, the body as a machine more than man-made creations as machines. "It's possible. She knew my tech savvy runs about as far as how to use my phone."

He grinned his regular, comforting grin, and Macey's heart seized. The skip of a beat nearly made her cough.

Trey laid a hand on her shoulder, which only intensified the feeling. "You okay, Mace?"

She nodded and bolted from the chair, the quick motion drawing pain from her side. "Swallowed wrong. Need something to drink."

But it was so much more than that. She went into the kitchen with her back to him, hoping against hope that he wouldn't follow, and pulled a pitcher of tea from the fridge.

Trey was the guy who had her back. The guy she trusted more than she'd ever trusted another man. The friend who'd grieved with her when Olivia died.

He was not heart-thumping material. He couldn't be. Because he wasn't interested in her, and if he found out she was skipping beats because of him, she might just lose his friendship forever.

EIGHT

"This is all way too easy." Dana Santiago sat at Trey's kitchen table with the alarm laptop and an array of devices Trey would never understand.

His backup had arrived in the late afternoon and had set straight to work. While Dana connected gadgets to the laptop and started searching, her fiancé and their teammate, Staff Sergeant Alex "Rich" Richardson, had helped Trey install Macey's new door, complete with a deeper-set dead bolt. Nobody would be kicking that door in anytime soon.

As far as Macey knew, Rich was a buddy who'd shown up to help with the door. If only everything could be so simple. It was close to midnight now and, while Rich sat on the back deck and kept an eye on Macey's house, Trey walked over to stand behind Dana and watch her work.

There were several open windows on the laptop screen and she aimed a finger at one in the top left. "Here there's a series of emails to a random address from a free email service, setting up drops along with some extremely detailed locations and package contents. Someone out there is still sending messages using this account, too."

"So they're still active?"

"If this is real, then *Macey* is very, very active."

"There's no way. I've been with her almost every evening and every weekend. I've surveilled her at work and even when she runs errands. There is literally nothing out of the ordinary about her." As much as the hard evidence said she was involved, the bigger picture pointed to an innocent woman. "Where are the emails from? Are they coming from this laptop?"

"I'll dig a little deeper, but I'm guessing a trace will land us in an infinite loop of rerouting until we can't determine where they originated." Dana indicated a window in the lower half of the display. "This is a whole string of texts to an overseas phone number that I'll guarantee is a burner. Some of them are recent but, again, they could be spoofed." The bottom left window held a web browser with the search history open. "And here? Web searches for high-dollar vacation homes and a million other ways to spend a large windfall of money."

Trey sank into the chair beside Dana, taking in all of the evidence. With just what was on the screen, they had enough to convict Macey and put her into maximum security for a very long time.

Yet, once again, it was all wrong. "No one is this sloppy."

"Most middle schoolers can cover their tracks online better than this." Dana pursed her lips and shrugged. "This is not how people who deal on the dark web and sell intel to the highest bidder operate. There would be coded messages and encryption. If this was real, it would be a slam dunk to put Macey Price away for life."

"So she's being set up." Someone else had to see it. He couldn't be the only one.

Dana sat back, ran her hands through her hair and then laced her fingers behind her head. It was a clear sign of frustration. "Unless Macey has an IQ in the bottom of the basement and the common sense of a squirrel crossing the road, then I'd lean heavily toward a setup."

Any relief Trey felt at having his own suspicions voiced by another person flamed out quickly. It was their job to uncover evidence and turn it over, not to make judgment calls. If whoever headed up prosecution on the government's side didn't see things their way, then Macey's life was over the instant they passed their findings on. "How long can we legally sit on this?"

Dana straightened and drummed her fingers on the table between the laptop and an external drive. "I'm still digging, so until I finish a thorough search, we're safe. I want to comb this hard drive, see if there's a partition that isn't obvious. Maybe whoever is behind this left a back door. If they did, we might be able to trace it to our real culprit."

Rich walked in Trey's back door and shut it, glancing at his watch. Tall and broad-shouldered, the former Special Forces soldier turned investigator cut a commanding presence. "Midnight, Blackburn. It's your watch."

Trey pushed away from the table. "All quiet?"

"Quiet, but not dark. Every light in that house is on." He crossed the room and flicked the laptop where Dana was working. "Speaking of sleep, you need some. The captain told me you were at the office until three this morning working on the Deering case."

It looked like Dana started to protest, but then she visibly deflated. "I guess this can wait a few hours. I'm liable to miss something without sleep." She looked up at Trey. "Where do you want me?"

"Guest room. Rich can take the bonus room over the garage. I know how he is about having the TV on at night."

"Yeah, that'll stop once we're married." Dana grinned and closed her laptop.

Trey snagged his phone and a water bottle off the island, then closed the back door behind him, giving the couple some privacy for their good-nights. It looked like they'd found the right stuff in each other, and while Trey was glad for them, it tugged at his own broken future.

He glanced at the door as he settled onto a deck chair. Then again, Rich had battled a horror story of broken dreams when his first fiancée was murdered. Somehow, he'd managed to love again.

It wasn't loving again that had Trey tied up in knots. It was trust. He glanced at a sky scattered with stars. "How is it that I can trust You and not..." His chin tilted down and his gaze leveled on Macey's dining room window. *And not her.*

Not any *her.*

He could blame God for what had happened with Gia, but no. She'd made her own choices and followed her own path. God had had nothing to do with her betrayal. For a while, Trey hadn't been able to say that, but then God had put the right person in Trey's path at the right time to pull him out of a pit that would have killed him otherwise.

A shadow passed Macey's window and Trey gripped the phone tighter. It was late. Did he dare?

Yeah, he dared. He pressed the screen and hit her contact number.

She answered before the phone rang once. "Shouldn't you be asleep?"

"Shouldn't you?" He propped his feet on the deck railing. "Your house is lit up like you're calling in 747s for a landing."

"Where are you?" The sound of her settling into the leather recliner came through the line. It was a familiar sound, one he'd heard a hundred times over the months. One that shouldn't bring him a measure of comfort, although it definitely did.

"Sitting on my deck. Couldn't sleep. Are you okay? You're sure you don't want me to crash on your couch?" Maybe if he did, she'd get some rest. If she was planning to return to work tomorrow, she was going to need it. He still questioned the commander's judgment on that one, but keeping her home would arouse suspicion. And surely the team watching her would be operators the commander trusted.

From inside Trey's house, Rich's footfalls came from the stairs and the sound of running water could be heard from the guest bathroom. Neither Rich nor Dana would miss him if he left, but they might have questions about how emotionally invested he was if he did.

Well, if Macey needed him, then they could question all he wanted. He really wasn't sure at this point what his answer would be anyway.

"I'm good. Eventually I'll probably pass out on the couch. But can I ask you a favor?" Macey's voice was warm and had settled into something different, almost like talking with him eased some of the tension in her vocal cords.

It made him feel strong in a way he hadn't felt since Gia had chosen another man, had walked away and left him an empty shell who questioned everything he'd ever thought himself to be.

"Trey?"

Great. She'd busted him thinking. "I'm here." His voice was too deep. There was something about sitting on his deck on a spring night and talking to Macey while knowing she was on the other side of those lights next door. It was personal. The darkness peeled the job away. The physical walls between them made his internal walls feel insignificant. "Do you need something?"

"It's dumb really." Her voice grew smaller.

Trey would do anything to make her feel like she was safe, even if it meant sleeping on the mat by her back door.

She sighed. "I'm home and everything is locked, but tomorrow I have to drive to work. It's so open, and I feel like, with all that's happened, I don't want to be totally alone. I should be stronger than that."

"There's a limit to what anyone can bear. Don't beat yourself up." She'd been through so much, and the physical assaults had to be taking a mental toll. He'd felt it himself when he'd returned from deployment and back to life on home soil. Overseas, he'd had a gun and a team to back him up. The first few times he'd driven alone down the road at home or been in public, he'd felt vulnerable and exposed, with no way to defend himself. Even Macey's own home wasn't safe. "What time do you need to be at work? My day's flexible. I can drop you off and pick you up."

"Thank you." This time the smallness in her voice was relief, not fear.

She *did* feel safe with him. Something cracked inside Trey. Something that left him breathless and dazed, maybe even a little scared. Something he hadn't even felt when Gia had agreed to be his wife.

This was soul deep and heart heavy.

"You're breathing funny. Are you okay?" Her voice came again, caressing his ear, gentle and caring.

He worked to regulate his breathing as he slid down into the chair. He really should get off the phone, but talking to her as he sat watch was infinitely better than sitting alone. "Just getting comfy. I feel like you're going to need to talk for a while."

"We don't have to."

"I want to. It's fine. I might as well talk to you as lie inside and stare at a dark ceiling, right?"

"Same here. Except my ceiling is apparently lit up like a runway."

He chuckled. "So, want to talk about the Stanley Cup playoffs? The fact that they're remaking your favorite '80s movie, and it's a total disgrace to all of humanity that they would even consider such an awful, awful thing?" He finished in a high-pitched whine, desperate to hear her laugh.

She rewarded him with a soft chuckle. "We've talked both of those to death. I'd rather talk about something else."

"Like what?"

"You."

The single word pierced his soul. He couldn't remember the last time anyone had personally asked about him.

He was in so much trouble. He'd have to be very careful with his answers. It was easy to forget she didn't know the real him. That her "Trey Burns" existed only for this op. "Sure." The word splintered on the emotion she'd loosed inside him. He took a long drink of water, nearly draining the bottle. "Fire away."

"I was just wondering, because I had a lot of time to kind of lie around and think today… What is it with you and hospitals?"

"What?" How had she landed there? And how had he let her?

"Most people hate them, but you? You were positively white today. It made me realize you're probably my closest friend in the world since Olivia died but I know nothing about you."

By design. Because he couldn't let her know who he really was. Because eventually he would be reassigned or she would find out he was an investigator and hate him for the rest of her life.

But until then, he'd give her what he could. He couldn't deny her.

And that might be his undoing.

Had she really asked him that question? Macey pulled the quilt that had once belonged to her grandmother over her head and burrowed deeper into the recliner. It had been on her mind all afternoon, but

really? He'd given her the easy conversational sugges-
tion of sports or movies and somehow she'd gone deep.
Her cheeks heated, and it wasn't from the warmth beneath the blanket, either. She opened her mouth to take
his offered way out and discuss hockey, but he'd already
started to speak.

"You're sure you want to go there?" His end of the
line shuffled as though he were settling in or sitting
taller, probably stressed out by her question. It was
hard to tell.

He'd offered another way to cut this conversation,
but the truth was, she didn't want to take it. She wanted
to know what had hurt him, wanted to somehow slay
the dragon that had wounded a man who typically stood
taller than any mountain she'd ever seen. It didn't seem
that anything should be able to make him look the way
he had today, uncertain and defeated. Scared. "You go
where you feel like going. You can talk about whatever
you want. I doubt either of us is sleeping tonight, so we
might as well talk." She pulled in a deep breath and
went for it. "But I really would like to know if you'd be
willing to tell me. It's up to how you feel."

"Well then, I feel like you need to open your front
door and let me in."

Macey's pulse jumped. The whole reason she'd denied him earlier was that looking him in the eye was
too hard when her emotions were jumbled up and completely confusing. But how could she tell him no when
he was standing on her porch, wanting to talk about
something that was obviously difficult for him? That
allowed her deeper into his life?

This was dangerous. Not for her life, but for her heart.

This crush she was nursing was going to get her into deep trouble.

But right now, she didn't care.

Macey stood and let the quilt pool at her feet, staring at the door. She ought to say no, but her feet moved on their own, and next thing she knew, she'd turned the dead bolt and pulled open the door.

On the other side of the glass storm door, Trey stood with his phone still to his ear. He spoke into it instead of directly to her, his eyes never leaving hers. "So I was married before. A long time ago."

Her mouth opened, then closed. His gaze was direct and honest and tinged with a pain she'd never seen before. Her fingers gripped her phone tighter, but then he glanced at the door handle. Oh yeah. It was locked. And it was foolish to stand there and stare at each other while they talked on the phone. Guess this conversation was happening face-to-face after all.

When she shoved the door open, Trey pocketed his phone and walked into the room the same way he had a thousand times before. Only this time was different. There was an air about him that said he was about to hand her something he'd been holding back, some truth about his history that he'd never shared before. Maybe because of the late hour or the stress of the past couple of days. Maybe because he'd saved her life twice. Macey had no idea, but she did know she wouldn't deny him the opportunity to unburden himself. She owed him that much and more, even if it turned her heart inside out.

Trey stepped over the quilt she'd dropped and settled on the couch, removed his phone from his pocket and rested it on the wide arm of the sofa. He stared at the dark TV screen and waited for Macey to resume her seat.

She eased her way into the recliner, careful of the stinging ache in her side, and pulled the quilt up to her chin, trying to shield herself from this new vibe she'd begun to pick up from him.

"So. Married?" It was hard to picture Trey married. Hard to picture him as anything other than…well, just Trey. She struggled to keep her voice level and surprise-free. Maybe his wife had died and that was why he'd answered her hospital question with a statement like that. "How long ago is a long time?"

Without looking at her, Trey picked at the seam of his blue jeans, near his knee. He flicked an imaginary piece of lint away. "Divorce was finalized five years ago, which is about how long I was married in the first place."

He was thirty-one now, so that made him a young married. A young married who'd had dreams and hopes and had loved someone enough to share them. A prick of jealousy stung, but Macey shoved it away and waited for him to keep talking. This wasn't about her. Not in the least.

"When I was deployed for the second time, she found someone she liked better than she liked me. Met him in a bar after I'd only been gone about two weeks."

"Trey." Macey's heart broke for him, and all of her own troubles seemed to dissolve. She'd had her house invaded and been injured by an assailant, but he'd almost literally had his heart cut out of his body, had been betrayed by someone he'd trusted with his life, with his name. "I'm so sorry. She sent you a letter while you were fighting a war? That's awful."

His laugh was sharp and laced with bitterness. "If only. That would have been easy. What she did was about a thousand times worse."

NINE

Seriously. What was he thinking? Macey had been through enough without dealing with his sob story. He should leave it at that and head back to his house, where he could watch with a safe distance between them.

But he'd opened this box and he was powerless to close it. Something about hearing Dana say she agreed Macey might be innocent had freed his tongue. The knowledge made him want to give something back for all of the months he'd been hiding his real life from her. Something real in a mountain of falsehoods. He couldn't tell her everything, but he could give her something.

The selfish part of him ached to spill this story to someone who hadn't been there and who would hear it with unbiased ears. Someone who didn't have to rescue him the way Captain Harrison had.

Someone who would simply care because they cared and not because they were obligated to.

He finally dared to look at her. She'd taken up a position in the recliner and pulled her grandmother's quilt up to her chin, her fists balled inside, from the looks of it.

But it was her eyes, wide-open and sympathetic, that completely undid him. "My ex-wife didn't just leave. She kept up the charade for over six months, sending care packages and letters, talking about reunions, like everything was normal. She was living large on the extra money that came from me being gone. I trusted her to pay our bills and follow the savings plan we had put together, but she didn't."

"I'm so sorry, Trey."

Sympathy was exactly what he didn't want, but from Macey, it soothed something inside him. "I got off the plane for the redeployment ceremony, and she wasn't there. Her best friend was. With an envelope stuffed with divorce papers." It had been years, yet it still hurt. Not the losing-her part, though. He'd grieved his marriage and had moved on with his life, as hard as that had been. But to admit he'd been a blind fool was still rough. Gia had stolen everything he'd had, from his money to his heart to his pride. And he'd been the idiot who'd missed it all.

"You're kidding." Macey's voice was as cutting as any blade Trey had ever used. She dropped the blanket and got up stiffly, favoring her injured side. She stood in front of the fireplace with her back to him. "I've heard of women doing terrible stuff like that, but I assumed it was some kind of military-wife urban legend. I can't imagine doing that to someone you're supposed to love and be committed to for life. I—" She bit off the words. "I'm sorry. That was hurtful."

"But true."

It took away some of the sting of his own clueless stupidity. Macey didn't blame him. She blamed the woman who'd wronged him. It was a novel idea. "You know that would be illegal." Ironic, since the whole reason he was in her life was criminal.

Criminal. He frowned. For a few minutes, he'd forgotten this was a job, but he couldn't stop talking now. She'd grow suspicious. He'd dug a hole he now had to make his way out of, and the only way to do that without tipping her off was to finish the story.

At least, that was what he told himself. "You're wondering what that has to do with the hospital."

Flexing her fingers, Macey turned, then shook her hands as though she was trying to talk herself out of taking a punch at the stone fireplace. She simply watched and waited.

Waited for him. Her friendship was a gift he didn't deserve, especially considering he'd initially befriended her to investigate her. Every day, though, he became more of the ally Macey had no idea she needed.

Sitting forward on the couch, Trey said, "I got a little self-destructive. I was young, hurt. Indestructible after two deployments. Summed up in one word, I was reckless." All things he'd never said out loud. Captain Harrison had watched it happen, so Trey had never had to discuss it. To admit his failings to another person was both difficult and unbelievably freeing.

"You don't have to talk about it."

But he did. This wasn't about Macey, after all. It was something he had to do if he was going to be truly whole again.

Telling Macey was safe, because there was nothing genuine to lose. Soon, he'd vanish from her life and move on to another case, leaving her to wonder what had happened to him. That cut almost as much as Gia's manila envelope had. "After that, I drifted. I mean, I stayed in the army, but I was following the routine and sort of sliding and not sure how to get my footing."

"That's hard to imagine." Macey's voice was low and intense, as though he was the only person in the world and what he had to say were the most important words ever spoken.

"That was pre-Jesus." Trey thanked God every day that Jesus had found him before he'd flamed out, even if the ride to that point had nearly destroyed him.

"Hmm." Hard to tell what that one short sound meant. Macey had never been big on Jesus, and he'd never forced it. Maybe that was one more reason she needed to hear this, or that God had made him feel the need to spill it out in all of its awful stench.

Trey pulled in a deep breath, bracing himself for the hardest part. "I was out with some buddies of mine. We were on a backcountry two-lane not far from Fort Drum. A couple of the guys decided they'd never tried drag racing before, so why not?" He could still feel the chill of the early fall New York night, could still see the dark ribbon of roadway that stretched straight into the distance for over a mile before curving to the right. Could still hear Drew Brace's challenge. Connor Wise's brand-new Mustang against Trey's six-year-old Charger, the one thing he'd managed to keep after the divorce.

Trey had tried to talk Drew out of it, but the man was insistent. The way the rest of the guys were egging him on, Trey's fight was in vain. He'd refused to drive, though he'd finally decided to ride shotgun, somehow foolishly thinking that would give him some sort of control if things went south.

Sometimes at night, he still woke up feeling the vibration of the engine as it poured through the passenger seat. Despite his reservations, it was an adrenaline high his numbed body and mind hadn't felt since deployment, a jolt of excitement he'd chased since his return. For the first time in a long time, he'd felt like a man.

The couch beside him shifted and Trey realized he'd been staring at his fingers, had forgotten Macey was in the room. It was an abrupt jolt, looking up to see her stone fireplace in front of him and not the bluish hue of dashboard lights and dark road. Her warm hand on his back felt so different from the leather seat and the crease of his jacket that had bunched up behind him that night. It was as though she sensed where this was going.

He told her everything, and her fingers dug deeper into his back with each passing word. The roar of engines and the squeal of the tires. The sudden swerve of the vehicle as Drew lost control and the explosive jolt as the Charger slammed into a pole and flipped forward.

The vehicle had been split by the pole—straight through the steering column and the driver's seat. Although, truth was, that was what others had told Trey. He'd remembered nothing after the initial hit.

Until he'd woken up to the lights of the trauma center in Syracuse.

He shrugged away from Macey's touch. The weight of her hand, even the weight of his clothes, almost physically hurt. "The only worldly possession I had left was destroyed. I busted some ribs and broke my leg. Weird thing really, considering how fast Drew was running. But Drew…"

"He didn't make it."

Trey shook his head. "That's the thing about hospitals. I can still smell it and see it and remember how it felt when my buddy came in and told me Drew was gone." He spared her the details that no one had spared him. Nobody should have to live with that image. Although, it had been the one that had jolted him out of apathy and self-centeredness. "So every time I have to walk into one, it all comes back."

"I'm sorry." She reached her arm around his back and laid her head against his shoulder, likely trying to offer comfort. "I am. That's awful."

All her touch did was remind him that he was a man who needed to be very careful where he trod. She was slowly sneaking away parts of his heart, parts she could never have, whether she was innocent or not.

He cleared his throat, but although he knew he should pull away, he didn't. Her comfort felt too warm, too right. "My former team leader was stationed a day's drive away, but I looked up on my first day in a regular room and there he was. I have no idea who told him."

Captain Gavin Harrison had pulled no punches and had called him out about throwing his life away, foolish behavior and how Trey was never going to find peace if he didn't give his life over to God, who'd made him in the first place. The commander was that kind of guy. He laid things right out there like they had to be.

"Because of him, I learned that Jesus sacrificed Himself on the cross for people like me. That I didn't have to be perfect. In fact, I needed to know I wasn't. And while

people can totally rip you up and wreck your trust—
and usually do—God's not like that. He might not do
things the way you'd like, but they always work out for
the best in the end."

Macey pulled away and shifted an inch or so down
the couch. "So Jesus is how you went from that—" she
waved her hand as if to gesture at something in the far-
off distance "—to this." With another flick of her wrist,
she indicated him, the new guy sitting in front of her.
Then she snapped her fingers. "Like that."

"Not like that. It took time. It took healing." Suddenly, the warmth and draw to Macey Price didn't
matter. Having her hear his story did. Having her understand what was missing in her life did. "It changed
everything for me."

She crossed her arms. "I'm fine, in case you hadn't
noticed."

Up went her walls. While he wanted to push, something deep inside urged him to let his story stand on
its own. God would do the work that Trey couldn't do.

He stood, reached for her hand and pulled her up
to him, wrapping his arms around her waist. At first,
she was stiff, but then her head tucked against his neck
and she relaxed.

He'd never touched her before, not like this. They'd
high-fived and done that side-hug thing, but this...

This was about to be his undoing.

He pressed a kiss to the top of her head, pulled away
while saying his goodbyes and walked out the door to
stand guard from a distance, praying he could protect
her from the danger in the darkness.

* * *

I'll be there in ten.

Macey stood in the center of the kitchen, phone in hand. Why had she asked Trey to drive her to work? She was a grown woman and had driven herself places since she was sixteen. Today should be no different. It wasn't like she was injured to the point of incapacitation. While her side itched and ached in a way that definitely wouldn't let her forget she was wounded anytime soon, she was perfectly capable of work and self-care. She was well versed in self-defense and—

But self-defense had been useless the day before.

Her pulse raced and her body broke into a sweat. That reaction had all of the markings of some real anxiety setting in. Anxiety that shouldn't surprise her. She'd been a victim twice. The odds of that were so long, they were practically inconceivable. What was to stop a third person from coming at her with thievery or murder or worse on their mind?

But was she any safer with Trey? The man made her feel. Made her remember long-ago dreams of white dresses and shared mornings and all of the things she shouldn't be dreaming about a man who would ultimately find someone better than she. He wasn't even romantically interested anyway.

After all, he'd kissed her on the head last night. The same way a guy would kiss his sister. Or his puppy. Everything pointed to a guy who saw her as…well, *one of the guys*. She was in the friend zone.

Macey poised her finger over the screen to text him that she would be fine on her own, that he could go on about his normal life without worrying about her, but of its own volition, her thumbs typed out OK.

Really?

She was so not okay.

It was too late to call him off now, though. If she retracted her consent, he'd be at the door trying to make sure she was safe and not being held at gunpoint.

Her heart rate spiked again. The way things were going, *gunpoint* might not be that far out of the realm of possibility.

Maybe it wouldn't hurt to have a bodyguard drive her to work after all.

Enough. This was ridiculous. She was starting to sound like her middle-school self crushing on Jared Riley. And look how that had ended. He'd called her out in front of their entire seventh-grade science class and had the whole room laughing at her.

She'd never been comfortable around a lab table again.

Stomping into her bedroom, Macey snatched her backpack off the floor and paid for it with a stab of pain from her side. *Slow down, girl. You'll hurt yourself for nothing.*

She forced herself to take a deep breath, gathered up everything she'd need for work and let Kito inside, where he'd spend his morning curled up in a sunbeam until she dashed home at noon to set him free for a quick run in the backyard.

That meant Trey would have to bring her back. Macey stopped in the middle of the living room, her backpack dangling from her fingers. He'd have to run back and forth for her all day. Maybe she should drive herself, after all, and let him—

His knock on the front door nearly sent her out of her skin. That was proof she wasn't in any condition to be driving.

She crossed the room and pulled the door open. "Hey, are you taking a lunch break today?" He frequently ran home from the post for lunch, claiming he'd rather spend money on gas than eat in the chow hall or the P/X food court.

Trey stepped back. "I was planning to. Why?"

For a second, Macey forgot why. The sight of him on her porch in his uniform jolted her all over again, as though she was seeing him for the first time and realizing that the God Trey believed in had done a mighty fine job of sculpting such a jawline.

She'd hoped whatever had flashed through her last night because of him would flash right on out again, but it seemed, instead, to have increased in intensity. She closed her eyes and exhaled. Her brain needed a decent night's sleep. Maybe then it would give up on this sudden idea that Trey might be her trustworthy soul mate.

Macey glanced up to find him looking at her expectantly, as though he could read her mind, but then she remembered he was waiting for her to finish her thought. Macey shook her head to clear it as she stepped out onto the porch. "Can you let Kito out at lunchtime? You should still have my spare key from yesterday." She set her backpack at her feet, then pulled her keys from her pocket and flipped to her house key, the everyday action grounding her into reality, at least for a second.

Trey picked up her backpack and slung it over his

shoulder as Macey turned to lock the door. "Anything you need, Mace."

Her hand froze with the key in the lock. Why did he have to say it like that? With his voice low, as though he knew her insides were more scrambled than the eggs she'd tried and failed to eat for breakfast.

Anything you need only lasted for so long.

But Trey said it like that because it wasn't some flippant response. He'd meant it. He was that kind of guy. The kind who truly would do anything for anyone.

The kind of guy who would do anything for her. He'd shown such concern for her repeatedly over the past few days. But he'd do that for any friend, right? "Trey?"

"Yeah?"

"Are we friends?" That wasn't what she'd meant to say. Clearly, they were friends. What she really wanted to know was *Are we friends or something more?*

Trey's head tipped forward. He was standing so close behind her that the movement brought his cheek close to her ear. For several seconds, Macey's breath stopped as he said nothing. He reached around her and laid his hand on hers where she still held the key in the lock, nearly embracing her.

If she turned her head slightly, so slightly, she might have her answer. But just as she decided to move, he seemed to shift into high gear, turning the key and lifting his head again.

He stepped around her and pulled the key from the lock, holding it out to her with a half grin on his face. "You know we are. Nobody else I know can quote me the NHL rule book during hockey games or make a mean homemade pizza. I think you're a keeper." He pressed his lips together tightly and shifted his gaze away from her. Then he turned and walked down the steps. "Let's go. I don't want you to be late because I'm distracted making up poetry about your pizza."

Her pizza. Sure thing. Pocketing her house keys, she followed him to his truck and climbed inside, *I think you're a keeper* running circles in her head and messing with her more than her own emotions ever had. The words didn't mean a thing, and the weight of that truth crushed the air from her lungs to the point she couldn't even speak for the entire fifteen-minute ride to her office.

For half a second on her porch, she'd thought he might feel the same way she was beginning to feel, that he might truly be the kind who stayed. She'd thought he might step in front of her and kiss her, tell her with his actions the words she wished he'd say. That she was more than a friend. That she was, in fact, *a keeper.*

Trey fidgeted the entire ride, tapping the steering wheel with his thumb, changing the channels on the radio and glancing at Macey, then back to the road when she caught his eye.

But he said nothing. It was almost as though he'd read her thoughts or picked up on her vibe and was embarrassed by her stupid emotions.

When he put the truck into Park in front of her office, all she wanted was to get out and away from him before she made an even bigger fool of herself. He'd clearly figured her out. She'd get Patricia or Anne to drive her home and shoot him a text later to say she didn't need him anymore, somehow make him doubt that she was feeling crazy things. "Thanks for the ride."

She shoved the door open and forced herself not to run up the walkway to the front of the building.

It was her day to open. She pulled her keys from her pocket and aimed for the door.

"Macey!" His call was punctuated by the sound of his truck door slamming and his footsteps practically running up the sidewalk behind her.

Couldn't he just leave?

He reached her before she could get the key into the lock. "You left your backpack in my truck." He sounded strangely out of breath, as though the sidewalk was two miles long and he'd sprinted the whole way.

Oh great. Her backpack. Because she needed another way to look like an idiot today. Steeling herself for one more look into those eyes of his, she turned to face him.

He was standing so close, her elbow brushed his stomach. He was looking down at her and his eyes registered the same shock that had just jolted through her own heart.

Macey moved to step back, but she was too close to the door. There was nowhere to turn away from this man and keep him from seeing what was surely written all over her face.

She didn't want to be his friend. For the first time in her life, she wanted to take the hand of another and see where it led them, maybe even to forever. She wanted to trust someone would stay by her side. No matter how much she wanted to look away, the force of her emotions pinned her into place.

Trey's eyes wandered her face in a gentle way she'd never seen before, one that melted even more of her heart. Finally, his gaze drifted to her lips, then back to her eyes.

Macey tilted her chin up to him. If he was offering…

With a sigh that almost sounded tortured, he breathed her name. Then his arms were around her and he pulled her close, tipping his head toward her and—

As abruptly as he touched her, Trey jerked his head to the side and stepped back, his expression almost pained. He shook his head slowly and everything about him screamed of regret.

"Mace, that was… We shouldn't…" He dragged his hand down his face. "This can't happen."

Without further explanation, he walked two steps back from her, then stopped, pulled her backpack from his shoulder and extended it to her. "I can't explain why. I want it to happen. It just can't." When her fingers closed around the strap, he turned and walked away. "I'll pick you up after work." The words floated back to her, heavy and troubled.

With trembling fingers, Macey let herself in through the glass front doors and walked straight across the lobby to the office, away from where he could see her from where he sat in his truck. She dropped her back to the wall and hugged her backpack to her chest.

He cared the same way she did. He wanted this as much as she did. He'd come so close and then ripped her to shreds.

Ripped…

And while people can totally rip you up and wreck your trust—and usually do—God's not like that.

Trey had used that same word when talking about

God the night before. Now he was the one to rip her up and wreck her trust.

She'd known it would happen. Should have steeled herself against him. Her mother couldn't be trusted. Trey couldn't be trusted.

She shoved away from the wall and straightened. Whatever. If she couldn't trust the people closest to her, how could she trust a God who was so far away?

TEN

Sitting at his desk, Trey dug his elbows into the wood and planted his palms against his temples. What had he been thinking? And what if her additional security detail had witnessed the whole thing?

He groaned and pressed his palms tighter to his head. He'd done a whole lot of foolish and impulsive stuff in his life, but almost kissing Macey Price was probably the second worst. It didn't matter that she was likely innocent. He was an investigator. Undercover. Supposedly emotionally detached.

Well, his emotions had been anything but detached this morning. They'd been fully engaged. It had been hard enough to step back on her front porch, and he'd thought he'd succeeded in keeping his heart tucked safely out of the way. But then she'd turned and with that look of wonder or whatever it was in her eyes…

He'd fallen into that look before he even realized he was moving. It wasn't about a kiss or a touch. That would have been easier to explain away. No. This was worse. This was about realizing in an instant that, yes, Macey Price really had become his friend. Worse, she was becoming something more. That she truly was *a keeper*. Why had he even said something as insane as that?

Because she brought out a peace in him, a feeling that he'd somehow been put back together again after war and divorce and stupidity had torn him into too many tiny shreds. It was a feeling that he might actually be of value to someone again. Important. Capable.

Capable? Maybe as a man but not as an investigator. If this was the real world and he was really just a soldier and Macey was really just his neighbor, this could be a real thing between them. They could explore the emotions behind that near kiss, could date, could maybe consider a future together.

He groaned and dropped his head lower. Marriage wasn't a thing he should ever think. Because this wasn't the real world, at least not for him. He was playacting.

And it was killing him.

"You kissed her, didn't you?"

The male voice from Trey's home office door jerked his hand and nearly dropped his head to the desk. Trey sat upright so fast his chair shifted a couple of inches back. "Don't you knock?"

"Nope." Rich walked in and dropped into a canvas camping chair Trey had once shoved into the corner. He dragged it to the desk and settled in like they had all day to run their mouths. "You need better furniture."

"This is temporary. It's an op. I have what I need to live for the few months I'm here." Exactly the thing he should have been telling himself this morning when he'd decided to make all sorts of unspoken promises to Macey. He winced.

"I'm guessing it doesn't feel so temporary right now."

Was Rich seriously trying to have this discussion? "Let's keep this to talking about the job, okay?" Trey planted his hands on the desktop and pushed himself up, then walked toward the door.

Rich stood, too, and stepped in front of him. His stance was loose, friendly.

But the action still felt threatening. Trey's spine stiffened and his shoulders drew back. "This is not about to turn into a fight, is it?"

"Nope. Because you aren't that guy anymore."

Trey exhaled his frustration. Rich was right. He wasn't the type to jump straight into a fight anymore, and this wasn't about his teammate anyway. Trey sank onto the edge of his desk and crossed his arms over his chest. Maybe he shouldn't keep this all to himself. Of all the people he knew, Rich was probably the most closely related to his situation. He'd met Dana while protecting her from an arms dealer with a vendetta against her birth parents. It wasn't necessarily an official duty like Trey's, but Dana had been cast out from her job with the US Marshals at the time. Somehow, they'd made it work. "This is different."

"Different than what?" Rich took his seat in the camp chair again and waited.

"Than you and Dana."

Exhaling loudly, Rich shifted his jaw to one side, as though thinking about what to say next. Trey was pretty sure he'd never seen someone actually "chew on their words," as his grandmother used to say.

Finally, his teammate nodded slowly. "Yeah, you're right. It's different." He looked up and pinned Trey with his gaze. "I don't know how you undercover guys do this."

"Neither do I."

"Maybe you're not cut out for undercover."

Trey winced with a pain that shot straight up from his gut. Someone had spoken his worst fear out loud.

But it was also his truth, the one he'd circled but never allowed to come full center. There was more than a little bit of shame that someone else had to voice it first. He wasn't sure what to do with it, either, so he simply waited for Rich to continue.

"I know I somehow got this rep for handing out wise advice or something—at least, that's what I've heard." Rich flashed a grin that faded quickly. "But when it comes to this, I've got nothing. I know in my case, it was tough to keep the job separate from the feelings. I'm guessing you've found the same problem."

What would happen if he had? What could he do about it? Those were the main questions.

The answers all amounted to *nothing*. There was nothing he could do, not in his present situation or in his present job. Trey dragged his hands back across the sides of his head. "If she was her and I was me—the real me…" Trey tossed his hands into the air and dropped them to the desk. "If she was definitely innocent—"

"She almost definitely is." Dana breezed into the room carrying her laptop, edged around Rich and shoved Trey to the side to settle her computer on the desk. "And I can prove it."

Trey jumped up and turned to face Overwatch's tech genius, who'd just become his second-favorite person in the world. "Bring it." If Macey was innocent and they could prove it, maybe when this was all over, he could finally tell her the truth and—

"Don't get ahead of yourself." Rich stepped closer to look over his shoulder, seeming to know exactly what Trey was thinking.

Well, Trey didn't want to hear it. He focused all of his attention on the laptop Dana had placed on his desk.

She pulled up a bunch of windows on her computer, where she'd installed the duplicate of the hard drive from Macey's house. "So, the drive was partitioned, just like you thought, Trey. Good catch." She tossed him a grin over her shoulder, then began to manipulate the track-pad. "But let's start at the beginning. The whole alarm system is set up almost the way Macey said it was. What she didn't know was that Olivia had a hidden master account and that Macey's user account is essentially useless. She can toggle a couple of settings on and off, but that's surface stuff. The gold is in Olivia's side of things." A few more clicks and she was in Olivia's account. The user interface was much different from Macey's.

Trey leaned closer, then whistled low. "So there really were pressure pads in the floor. Macey was joking about that and had no idea how true it was."

"Pressure pads, heat sensors, motion detectors… Olivia had a state-of-the-art security system. I'm not joking when I say the *Mona Lisa* would probably be safer in Macey's living room than it is in the Louvre."

"Why?"

Rich chuckled. "We all know why. That girl was hiding something big and she wanted to know every little goings-on inside her house. Even what her roommate was doing. If Macey became suspicious and snooped, Olivia wanted to know."

"Exactly. And just before she died," Dana added, "she upgraded. Even the yard has motion and heat sensors. Based on her schematics, I can give you approximate locations, but I don't know how she's hidden them. We can look later, but all of that is really just the introduction." She clicked back to Macey's account. "Here's where the fun begins. We have the email account buried under Macey's username full of dates and bank accounts and everything you'd possibly need to put our girl away for the rest of her life in some serious maximum security lockdown."

Trey's heart dropped clear to his boots. "Let's get to the innocent part."

"Trust me." Dana stopped everything and turned to face Trey head-on. "Macey is definitely innocent. Or, as we've said before, she's an idiot. And we both know she's not." She laid a hand on his forearm and held his gaze long enough to let Trey know she'd picked up on the same truths about his feelings as her fiancé had.

Great.

But his humiliation was momentary. Macey was innocent and Dana could prove it.

"Now that we've had the dramatic buildup, let's talk about where dear ol' Olivia made her fatal mistake." Always with the flair for drama, Dana skittered the mouse to the same system window Trey had explored before, the one with the unexplained large files. "Olivia installed cameras that Macey didn't know about. Cameras that were motion activated and, oh yeah, picked up sound. And then our extremely helpful friend clearly forgot she was effectively surveilling her own self. Now, I've just started going through the videos, and most of them are generic household stuff, but this one here is particularly interesting. It's from the week before Olivia died. I've cued it up to the best part."

With another click, Dana opened a file, and a video player took over the screen, frozen on a shot of Olivia standing in the living room, talking to a man who sat on the sofa, his back to the camera. Dana hesitated with her finger over the trackpad. "Y'all ready for this?"

Trey was ready for this weeks ago. It was all he could do not to shove Dana to the side and press Play himself.

When Dana ran the video, Olivia's familiar voice flowed from the speakers. "What happened to you never coming to the house?"

The man sat back on the sofa and rested his ankle on his knee as though this was a mere social call. "You wanted me to set up the NIC. I can't do that from a distance."

NIC—the network interface card Trey had found on the laptop. Olivia hadn't installed it. Her mystery guest had. So who controlled it now?

Olivia's voice droned on. "Do it quick and go. Macey thinks you're dead. If she happened to come by for something…" Olivia reached down and gave Kito a quick pat on the head. He leaned against her leg and eyed the man as though not sure he trusted him.

Olivia chewed at her lower lip for a moment, a shadow seeming to cross her expression. "I feel a little bad about throwing her under the bus this way." Her eyes hardened and she straightened. "But if we get found out, then we can't go down for this. It has to be Macey. They have to believe she's the one who's behind this."

"You've made sure to point everything to her."

"Everything. It's all coming together. And when the heat dies down in a few months, we'll have everything we've dreamed about for so long. Even your brother won't be able to stop it."

The man on the couch rose and walked to Olivia, pulling her into his arms. The rest of the conversation was unintelligible murmurs, but when the man turned his face toward the camera, Trey's entire body prepared to fight.

They had everything they needed to save Macey and to put an end to Sapphire Skull.

Jeffrey Frye was alive, and he was working hard to make sure that Macey faced the punishment for his crimes.

Macey dropped into the chair behind the reception desk and rested her hand gently on her side. It throbbed and stung, most likely from all of the work she'd done with her patients today. It was a good pain, though. She was alive and moving and out in the world. After a couple of days feeling like a victim, it felt better than amazing to have some control over her life again.

Tonya, the office manager, walked around the corner and stopped with her hands on her hips when she saw Macey. "Slacking off on the job?" She grinned and hip-checked the back of the chair as she walked by. "You've worked like a fiend today. Thanks for helping carry the load for Kenzie."

"Happy to." Not only had it kept her busy, Macey

had been happy to step in for the eight-months-pregnant therapist. "How's she doing?"

"She's feeling better now. She said their wide-open drive to the hospital today was a trial run for the real thing. Those Braxton-Hicks contractions can be pretty convincing." Tonya leaned back against the desk beside Macey and crossed her arms. "I'd have loved to have seen Phillip racing around trying to put everything together, though. I'm sure the panic was most definitely real."

Macey grinned. The tall, slim army ranger was usually in full control, but when it came to his wife's pregnancy, all of that *hooah* soldier stuff went right out the window. "We should have Kenzie wear a body cam on the way to the hospital when the real day comes. They could be an online sensation and earn enough money to put their baby through college someday."

Arching an eyebrow, Tonya nodded. "Good plan." She rose and glanced around the room. "Is everyone else gone for the day? And shouldn't you have left early? You opened this morning, didn't you?"

"I had a friend drive me here today. I've got about ten minutes before he gets here." Macey hadn't explained to anyone at work what had been going on. It all sounded so unreal, and she really didn't want all of the attention or to have to rehash the story over and over again. If any one of her colleagues found out she'd been slashed with a box cutter...

Macey shuddered and swallowed a wave of nausea. Maybe letting Trey drive her to work hadn't been such a bad idea. Except for that one moment. She'd managed to go the whole day not thinking about what might have been a kiss. Well, not with the front of her mind. The back had been spinning it on replay until she thought she'd sink into it and never come out again. He'd walked away, and that was all she needed to know.

"You still don't look so good. Glad tomorrow's Saturday. You can take the weekend off and recover from whatever knocked you off your feet the past couple of days. With a full load today, you might have overdone it."

If only recovery would come with rest. Sure, her body felt like it'd been hit by a truck, but it was going to take more than a couple of days off to heal her bruised emotions. "It was good to be back at work." Truer words were never spoken.

Glancing at her watch, Tonya stood and pointed to her office at the rear of the building. "I've got some phone calls to make about some patient referrals, so I'll be in my office. I'm looking to hire a new cleaning crew for the building since Michelle's husband is getting transferred to Fort Rucker. The new guy is going to stop by tonight or tomorrow, so if he shows up and you're still here, can you let him in and come get me? His name is James."

With a thumbs-up to Tonya, Macey turned in the chair and logged on to her user account to update her last patient's progress, more than a little relieved that she wouldn't be totally alone in the building while she waited for Trey. Charting gave her something to do that would stop her from thinking about the pain Trey's actions had wreaked in her chest.

Up the long hallway, Tonya's door clicked shut.

Macey planted her elbow on the desk and her chin

on her fist and stared out the front glass doors at the parking lot. If she'd been less busy today, she'd have waved Trey off and called a ride-share service.

Rather than replay his actions this morning, she focused on his story from the night before. His ex-wife's betrayal had been brutal. It was bound to be something he still battled. Maybe his walking away this morning wasn't about Macey at all. Trust was a big thing with him, and he'd said as much about God. He trusted God but not people.

Macey trusted neither. The people she could see couldn't be counted on. How in the world could she trust a God she couldn't see?

Pressing her palms against her eyes, Macey let the darkness swirl. Trey had been able to see his wife and look her in the eye, and she hadn't been trustworthy. Her treachery had left Trey bruised and broken.

What did Macey do now? The last thing she wanted to do was to lose his friendship, even if it could never grow into anything more. Pursing her lips, she pulled out her phone and fired off a text. She'd head him off before he arrived and she had to look him in the eye.

We've been friends too long to let something stupid make it all awkward. Pretend it never happened?

Hopefully, he'd see it before he saw her. And hopefully it would be enough to salvage their friendship.

Outside, a green sedan slowed to a stop at the end of the sidewalk and a tall man with a military haircut stepped out.

Macey shoved away from the desk with a sigh and

went to open the door for Tonya's new cleaning crew. She'd have to find a way to address everything with Trey, to have a conversation that would at least make him believe she was okay with their near kiss leading nowhere.

She turned the key in the lock and shoved the door open, holding it for the man. "James?"

He stopped halfway up the short sidewalk, his foot sliding as though he was surprised to see Macey standing there. For a second, he regarded her with a look somewhere between confusion and anger, but then he seemed to come back to himself and gave her a small smile. "Yeah. I'm James." He stopped just short of the door. "And you are…?"

"Macey. Come on in. You can wait in the lobby and I'll get Tonya for you."

He gave her an odd smirk, then nodded. "Tonya's still here?"

Something about him gave Macey an odd chill, almost like fingers walking up her spine.

She shook it off. After the way her week was going, she'd probably be suspicious of any male who stepped within ten feet of her. Sooner or later, she had to get over this freaky paranoia. "In her office. She wasn't sure if you were coming today or tomorrow."

With a brief nod, he brushed past her into the waiting room and walked over to the reception desk, speaking over his shoulder. "Had some time tonight. Thought I'd go ahead and take care of everything now. You said she's in the back?"

"Yep. I'll get her for you." Macey glanced into the

parking lot. Still ten minutes until Trey was due. Surely she'd be able to think of something to say by the time he—

A soft sound came from behind her and a hand clamped over her mouth as an arm snaked around her neck and drew her back against a heavy chest.

She struggled and fought to scream, digging into the arm with her fingernails, twisting and turning as tears sprang to her eyes and her air gradually closed off to the pressure against her throat. She jabbed with her elbow and hit air, tried to throw her weight forward, but he'd planted himself too firmly, ready to counter her every move. Her side pulled and ached.

A whisper blew hot against her ear. "Knock it off. I already know you're a seasoned fighter. You go quietly or I find whoever Tonya is and put a bullet in her head."

Macey whimpered and froze, then fired a silent prayer to the God Trey believed in. *Please. Please don't let Tonya come out here.* She slumped. The pressure against her throat made it hard to breathe. The pain in her side drove tears to her eyes. Fear pounded her heart against her rib cage. Even if she wanted to fight, she was powerless to do so, paralyzed by terror.

"Tell me where you put the intel. We paid for it in good faith." His grip on her neck tightened and spots danced before her eyes.

Her mind spun. Intel? Payment? The words didn't make sense. They fogged and scrambled as her body slipped into survival mode. She blinked and struggled to stay on the surface as darkness threatened to creep in.

The man dragged her toward the door. "Fine." His hoarse whisper grated against her ear, barely penetrating the fog. "You can come with me. I have some good friends who know exactly how to make you tell us what we want to know."

Macey's breath stuttered on the edge of a sob. Nothing made sense. Nothing. His words… She had to be dreaming. This had to be a nightmare.

The world grayed around the edges. Her ears deafened her with a roar she could no longer fight off.

There was no help coming. And she was about to die.

ELEVEN

Macey is innocent. Macey is innocent.

Trey wrapped up a quick debrief with Macey's new daytime security detail in a parking lot around the corner from her office and shifted his truck into gear, heading out to pick her up.

Macey is innocent. Macey is innocent.

Trey's heart pounded the same rhythm it had picked up when Dana made her pronouncement just two hours earlier. Relief had lifted weight from his shoulders, made him feel like he could stand taller. Maybe even breathe easier.

The back of his mind cautioned that this changed nothing between them. But at least now, when he left her behind to move on to his next assignment, he could be assured that she wouldn't go to jail for crimes someone else had committed in her name.

His relief blew away on a hurricane of anger. Olivia had betrayed Macey in a way no one should ever be betrayed. She'd toyed with Macey's life, putting her not only in danger of federal prison for the rest of her days but also in danger of those days being cut short by someone Olivia had clearly double-crossed. Someone who now wanted Macey dead.

The team's job had shifted. Captain Harrison had ordered them to protect Macey at all costs while searching for whomever was trying to destroy her. To find out what that person was searching for and to shut them down for good. Clearly, even though Olivia was dead, someone believed her pipeline of information was still wide-open and would stop at nothing to get what they wanted, even if it meant plowing Macey six feet under the ground.

The question was who. Jeffrey Frye was alive—or at least he had been on that video with Olivia—and he was clearly part of the plot against Macey. It was possible he wanted to finish what Olivia had started. Or had his brother Adrian bought the lies and was now seeking what they thought Macey possessed? Worse, was it an unknown actor? Someone they had yet to identify?

Dana was working every angle, but it would take time. Tracking down the living dead was a tall order.

The trick now was to figure out how to protect Macey twenty-four hours a day without her figuring out what was going on. This was still an undercover mission. And the longer she was kept in the dark about the danger she was in, the more likely they could get her through this without her ever learning that she'd been betrayed not only by Olivia, but by Trey, as well. As much as he'd like to rush her into hiding or into protective custody, they couldn't. Such a move could prevent them from ever ending this for good.

He whipped the truck around the corner into the parking lot. Keeping constant eyes on her was key. It was the only way to ensure those men never reached her.

He rounded the slight curve in the driveway at Macey's work and slowed to a roll. A green sedan sat at the curb in front of the sidewalk, two wheels up on the grass. Only one other car sat on the far side of the parking lot, a small red crossover with a stick-figure family in the rear window.

Where were all of Macey's coworkers? Why was the parking lot empty?

And whose sedan was that?

Something was definitely not right.

The glass doors to the building flew open and a man backed out, dragging a woman with him.

Macey.

Adrenaline revving into high gear, Trey fought the urge to gun the engine, opting for the element of surprise. He slid the truck into Park and eased out, leaving the door open and the engine on. He was running across the parking lot before he even had a fully formed plan. All he knew was that Macey was in danger and he was the only one who could save her.

The man dragging Macey down the sidewalk battled to hold on to her while simultaneously attempting to keep an eye on the surrounding area and any threats headed this way. He appeared to struggle with her as he covered her mouth and tried to drag her with him. An outline below his shirt at his lower back clearly showed a pistol tucked there.

Trey ran at full speed. He had one chance to take the guy down before he saw Trey and took his panic out on Macey or reached for that gun.

He prayed Macey didn't get hurt in the melee.

When they cleared the building, Macey threw her weight backward and twisted her shoulders, throw-

ing the man off balance. As he stepped sideways, Trey
dipped low and dug his shoulder into the guy's hip,
driving all three of them to the ground.

Macey grunted, rolled to her side and lay still.

The man tried to flip onto his back to fight, but Trey
had the height and strength advantage. He drove a fist
into the side of the guy's head and knocked him face-first
into the ground. Trey leaped onto his back and pinned his
face in the dirt with one hand while reaching for the handcuffs on the back of his belt under his shirt with the other.

With a moan, Macey rolled onto her back and stared
at Trey, wild-eyed and terrified.

"Get inside. Now. Lock the door and don't open it
for anyone but me, no matter what you see." He hauled
her attacker's arms behind his back and cuffed them
tightly, then pulled the gun from the dude's waistband
and tossed it about twenty feet behind him.

Macey continued to stare, motionless. "Now, Macey.
Now!" He hated to shout at her, but if this guy had friends,
things were going to get ugly fast. She was safer inside.

As she edged back toward the building, her eyes
never left the handcuffs Trey had shackled around the
man's wrists. She slipped inside and stood at the door,
staring and shaking.

The man bucked. Trey pinned his head to the ground
again, turning away from Macey's horrified gaze. No
matter what he did from this point forward, Macey
knew she was in danger.

Even worse, she knew the depths of Trey's lies.

She must be dreaming. She had to be. There was no
way the events of the past hour had been real.

Sliding her hands forward on Trey's kitchen table, she stretched out her arms and dropped her head to the cool wood. Her side ached and burned. The pounding pain in her neck and throat testified to the truth that the past hour had very much happened. A man had grabbed her. Threatened her. Tried to drag her away to tortures unknown.

And Trey… He'd taken the man down and hand-cuffed him. Two men in an SUV had raced in and hauled the man who'd attacked her away. Men who weren't police but who had clearly known Trey very well.

Once again seeming to know he was needed, Kito crept under the table and nudged Macey's thigh with his nose. She dropped a hand to his neck fur and buried her fingers there, grateful someone had thought to bring her precious companion to her. For a brief moment, with his blue eyes looking deeply into hers, she sank into a sense of peace.

It was short-lived. Her dog could give her comfort, but he couldn't give her answers.

"Here." There was a soft thud on the table near her head. A presence followed the female voice as someone slid into the chair beside her. "Water won't make everything better, but it will help."

Macey turned her face toward the voice, but didn't lift her head or pull her hand away from Kito. It was as though her body had given up the fight and was determined to melt the bones right out of her. Clearly, it had taken her emotions along with it, because she was completely empty. Dead and cold. Unable to feel even the terror she knew lurked somewhere inside her waiting to pounce.

She looked past the glass of ice water condensing droplets onto the table and met the brown-eyed gaze of Trey's friend Dana, a woman who'd greeted them at the door with a look of compassion and understanding. A woman she'd never seen before. Surely, Trey didn't have a girlfriend he'd never mentioned.

Then again, he'd cuffed a man in front of her, so how well did she really know him? "Who are you?" Her voice came out on a croak that would probably last a few days.

The woman graced her with a soft smile and leaned slightly closer, her long dark hair falling over her shoulder to swing near her cheek. She laid a warm hand lightly on Macey's back near her aching neck. "I'm someone who's been where you are right now."

Macey's eyes slid closed. Cryptic. Too cryptic. Maybe she really was dreaming. Maybe she'd been deprived of oxygen for too long. People talked in riddles or acted... well, not like themselves. Trey had practically thrown her into his truck and raced home, one hand gripping hers as he talked through his Bluetooth about things she couldn't hear over the whirlwind in her brain and in her life.

When they'd arrived at his house, he'd ushered her inside so fast she hadn't had time to protest that she wanted to go home. He'd pulled her to his chest, holding her close for a long time before handing her over to this woman with only a name.

Now he was somewhere in the house. The low murmur of his voice drifted up the hall. Macey desperately wanted him to come back and hold her again because, in that moment, in his arms, she'd felt safe and protected. Given what she'd seen and experienced, she shouldn't have, but she definitely did.

The shiver started deep inside her, somewhere she couldn't identify, and worked its way out to her fingers. She pulled her hand from Kito, who lay on her feet, and wrapped her arms around her stomach.

Dana got up and came back with a blanket that she draped around Macey's shoulders.

Macey sniffed when she recognized the blue material, a sudden rush of tears threatening. She swallowed them even though it hurt. "I bought this for Trey for Christmas." He carried that St. Louis Blues blanket to her house every time he came over to watch hockey. A few times, he sat on one end of the couch while she sat on the other, the blanket covering both of their laps, even though they never touched.

Dana sighed but said nothing. Instead, she reached out a slender finger, swiped a bit of condensation from the table and then wiped it on her jeans. A diamond ring glistened on her finger. Maybe that was why Trey had backed away. "Are you engaged to Trey?" Why else would this woman be in his house, touching his things? The thought ached in her heart more than the strain ached in her throat.

This time, Dana laughed out loud. It was short-lived but packed with humor that was totally out of place. "No. I'm engaged to Rich, the guy who helped Trey hang your door last night."

With what felt like the last of her strength, Macey pushed up from the table and sat back, sagging against the chair. She pulled the blanket tighter around her shoulders and angled toward the Dana woman, who reminded her a bit of some Lewis Carroll character in Wonderland.

Maybe that was it. She'd fallen through the looking glass.

"Can I go home?"

"How about we wait a few minutes? I think Trey wants to talk to you first." Dana slid the glass closer to Macey. "And I do, too. I meant what I said. I've been where you are."

Something inside Macey snapped. The fear and confusion all erupted and exploded on this stranger who claimed to know what she was going through. There was no way anyone could understand. "You've been attacked by strange men and don't know why? Had your house broken into? Been stabbed by a guy wielding a box cutter?"

A sad smile lifted one corner of Dana's mouth. "My threat was knives, not a box cutter. Many, many knives."

Macey straightened. There was no way this woman was telling the truth.

Or was she?

Dana sat back and crossed her arms, her eyes haunted in a way that couldn't be faked. "I used to work for the US Marshals Service in WitSec. The long and short of it is that someone wanted revenge on my birth parents, so they came after me."

She held her hands out in front of her and ticked off items on her fingers. "I was almost kidnapped from a friend's wedding, attacked in my own apartment, held at knifepoint more than once…" She stopped and lowered her hands to the table, staring at them as though they had her story written between her fingers. "It was a rough time. But in the midst of it, I found Rich. Sometimes, these things come with a silver lining. Rarely, but sometimes. Too often in WitSec there were no upsides to situations like ours. But sometimes…" She arched an eyebrow and shrugged. "There are times when God steps in and brings a blessing you never saw coming."

God again. First Trey, now this stranger who shared her story. With two women who'd been traumatized and terrorized sitting at the same table, it was hard to believe God was looking out for them. "Y'all keep bringing Him up. I just don't see it."

"Look at the positive instead of the negative. You're alive and safe here. You're beside someone who knows exactly what you're going through and can help you. Your home is intact. I'd say God's been pretty busy on your behalf."

"Maybe." It was too much to think about. The idea of some all-knowing, all-supreme being up in Heaven watching over her wasn't where her radar wanted to go. "That man at work… He thought I had something of his. He threatened to—" Macey swallowed bile that tried to rise in her throat and waited for her voice to cooperate. "He threatened to torture me. I have no idea what he's talking about. All of these things are connected, aren't they?"

She turned toward Dana and grabbed the woman's forearm with both hands, trying to hold on to reality the only way she knew how. "I wasn't randomly attacked. Somebody thinks I'm someone else. Or they

think I have something they want." Her heart rate accelerated and her words came faster as her fingers dug tighter on Dana's arm. "If I knew what it was, I'd give it to them. I'd give them anything they wanted. I'd—"
She sucked in a quick breath, released Dana and turned her face to the ceiling, shouting raggedly at a God she wasn't certain existed. "Just give me an answer if You are really up there!"

"I can give you some of those answers."

Macey blinked twice.

She saw Trey standing in the living room at the entrance to his hallway. A familiar face. A safe face.

A face she could trust in a sea of strangers and uncertainty.

She was on her feet before she knew it, and Kito leaped up with her, leaning against her leg. Her muscles wanted desperately to fling her body at Trey, but she was caged in by the wall on one side and by Dana on the other.

And by the expression on Trey's face before her.

She froze, planting her fists on the table for balance. He somehow managed to look like her friend and a stranger all at once. The look on his face was different, all angles and firm jaw. All business. No warmth.

Macey glanced from him to Dana, then to Rich, who had walked in to stand beside Trey.

They were conspiring against her somehow; she could feel it. There was danger somewhere—if not in this room, then lurking right outside the door.

Her head turned, seeking a way out. Her gaze zipped from the front door to the back door to the hallway. She was trapped. Blocked. Someone wanted to hurt her and now even her closest friend seemed to be a completely different person. Her breaths came in spurts. Her pulse skyrocketed. The room narrowed on Trey's face.

His lips moved. "Dana." There was panic in his voice as Macey's knees weakened.

Dana leaped up and grabbed Macey's arm. She turned her and shoved her into the chair, driving her head between her knees. "Breathe. Slowly. On my count. In… Out… You're hyperventilating. In… Out…"

Fighting for control, Macey focused on the gentle voice. *In… Out…* Over and over until her focus returned and her body stopped rebelling. She shrugged off Dana's hand and straightened. Humiliation and embarrassment heated her cheeks. She'd lost control in front of Trey and two strangers. What was happening to her?

Carrying a large tablet, Trey crossed the room warily and slid into the chair across from Macey while Rich stayed where he was near the hallway, looking like he wasn't exactly sure where he should stand.

Macey focused on Trey, her friend.

But was he really her friend?

Slowly, he laid the tablet facedown on the table and let his gaze capture hers. For a long moment, he simply looked at her, a number of emotions crossing his face too fast for Macey to interpret any of them. Finally, he glanced down at the tablet, then at Dana, then sat taller, his expression an impassive mask. "Macey, I need you to be strong right now."

She dipped her chin and wove her fingers into Kito's neck fur under his collar. Whatever he was about to say, her whole world was going to change. There was no doubt.

"I need you to be strong because…" Trey pulled in a deep breath and wouldn't let her look away from him. "Because almost everything you know about your life is a lie."

TWELVE

"I don't understand." Macey tightened her grip on Kito's collar and held on as though her dog could get her through anything. He protested with a soft whimper and pulled free, then walked under the table and dropped heavily by Trey's feet with a loud sigh.

Even her dog was against her.

She closed her eyes and dug deep, finding an inner strength she knew was there but had half feared had fled, never to return. When she opened her eyes, everyone was staring at her. "You're scaring me, Trey."

"I really don't want to, but this is scary stuff." He tapped his index finger on the rugged case around the tablet, then slid it across the table to Dana. "You do it." Shoving away from the table, he paced to the front window and stared at the tightly closed blinds, his fists clenched at his sides.

Whatever was going on, it was bad. Worse than she'd originally thought.

With a sigh, Dana pulled the tablet closer and popped the stand out of the back, then set it between herself and Macey on the table. She accessed the device with her thumbprint and flicked open a window.

The face of the man who'd attacked her only an hour earlier filled the screen.

Macey turned her eyes away as a chill racked her body. When it passed, she dropped her hand to her side and snapped her fingers.

Kito came closer and shoved his head against her palm.

She absently rubbed the soft fur of his ear. "Who is he? And why do you have his picture?"

For a long moment, Dana was silent. Then she clicked her tongue against her teeth. "Macey, I'm a government contractor. I consult for a military intelligence unit unofficially known as Eagle Overwatch. I do a lot of tech work and cyber investigating for them."

"Never heard of them." She'd grown up near Fort Bragg. Her soldier father had moved them there and then left them behind. "Sounds like something you made up."

"It's fairly new and I can't tell you much about it, but Overwatch steps in when normal military intelligence and investigations either hit a dead end or are being surveilled themselves. We were called in to investigate someone who could be working on the inside, someone who was stealing intelligence and selling it on the dark web to the highest bidder. Someone who was working closely with a group known as Sapphire Skull."

Macey sucked in a breath. Sapphire Skull had once made the national news. They'd blown up a government building and supply depot. Why was Dana sitting beside her talking to her about stolen secrets and Sapphire Skull? Why was—

The man's words rushed her memory. *Tell me where you put the intel. We paid for it in good faith.*

She gasped and turned to Dana, shaking her head violently from side to side. "No. No. No. I don't have any intelligence. That man…" She jabbed her finger against the tablet screen. "That man wanted to know what I did with the intel. I don't know. I mean…" She turned in the chair and her gaze found Trey's. "I don't know what or who, but I— Where would I even get those things? I don't even know any government secrets. I'm a physical therapist, not a spy." Why was she telling Trey this? He was her neighbor. Her friend. Not investigating her. Not like this Dana woman. And probably Rich, too. She poked at the tablet again and her finger slipped along the screen.

The photo changed, and Macey jerked.

Olivia's face, taken from her government ID, stared back at her.

Macey's hand dropped to the table and she sank against the back of the chair. "Why do you have Olivia's picture?"

Dana pulled the device out of Macey's reach and turned toward Trey, seeming to shoot him a silent plea for help. There was an intense, wordless conversation before he finally exhaled loudly and came to sit across from Macey. He took the tablet Dana had shoved toward him.

He stared at the screen, then looked up to meet Macey's gaze. "Olivia was…" He exhaled loudly and shook his head. "She was the one stealing secrets. It appears she was paid a monthly retainer by members of Sapphire Skull to pass along any data she deemed important. And she passed a lot of data."

Macey pressed her fingers to her lips and stared at Trey. The words didn't compute. Her roommate. Her best friend. A criminal? She'd lived with a criminal?

She'd be sick if everything in her hadn't suddenly shut down and gone numb, denying the truth she was hearing. Her emotions hit a wall and landed in an icy cold place where only words existed. No feelings. Just words. "Did they use her intel?"

From across the room, Rich spoke. "A supply warehouse in Texas. A small IRS satellite office in California. About half a dozen smaller nuisance attacks on government sites around the country have been traced back to her leak."

Two government employees had died in the IRS office. Several had been injured in Texas. And Olivia had sat beside her and watched the news like nothing was unusual in their lives. Like it was background noise. Just something happening in another state.

Macey sighed and searched Trey's face for the truth. "She really did that?"

He hesitated, then nodded. "She did. But there's… there's more." He flicked the tablet and stared at it for a long moment. "Her main contact was a man named Jeffrey Frye. He and his brother are the driving force behind Sapphire Skull. They're a couple of anti-government domestic terrorists out to make a name for themselves. And…" He turned the tablet toward Macey.

Only the man's profile was visible in a grainy surveillance photo, but there was no doubt as to who it was.

"That's Jeff Washington. Olivia's boyfriend." Maybe this was all a mistake. Maybe… She jumped to her feet. "Maybe Jeff coerced her. Maybe he stole stuff off her laptop or he—"

"We have a paper trail. Money, emails, documented meetings. But, Macey…" He flicked the screen again and a photo of Jeff with another woman popped up. Only the back of her head was visible, but Macey recognized the location. The hotel lobby where they'd stayed in Denver. He was handing Macey the purse Olivia had left behind after they'd all had dinner together on their last night in the city.

If she didn't move, she was going to be sick or explode. She looked down at Dana. "I need out. I need…I need out." Dana shoved the chair in and Macey squeezed past her, pacing to the kitchen and back, then to the front window where Trey had been standing moments before. "I'm on camera exchanging something with a terrorist." She lifted her eyes to the ceiling. "That wasn't Olivia's purse, was it? That was something else."

"Probably. Or it was an effort to make it look like you were involved." Dana spoke up from her seat at the table. "We don't have proof, but we do have this photo and others like it. The emails and bank accounts were all in your name."

"What?" Macey whirled toward Trey. He was her friend, right? Her ally? He knew her, knew she wouldn't do something like this. "I didn't do this. I wasn't a part of this. I didn't know anything." She strode to Trey and stood over him. "You know me. You know I didn't do this. I wouldn't do this."

Trey stood and reached for her, then stopped halfway and shoved his hands into his pockets instead. "I know. We all know. As of this morning, you're cleared."

"As of this morning? What happened this morning?" *Cleared?* She was *cleared?* Up until a few hours ago they'd honestly believed she could do something so heinous? Her mind spun. Her thoughts refused to gel.

Trey pulled his hands from his pockets and guided Macey into the chair. He handed her the tablet with a video playing. Olivia and Jeff in their living room. Talking about her. Framing her. As though she was nothing more than a pawn.

Using her and throwing her away like a dirty paper towel.

Her roommate. Her friend. Willing to destroy her life to save her own. No, actively working to destroy Macey's life to save her own.

"It can't be true." Stuff like this happened in movies. Or to strangers on the news. Not to her.

"I'm afraid it is." Trey looked down at her with sympathy and maybe even a bit of pity.

Her eyes narrowed and she stood, then took a step away from him. She crossed her arms and looked him up and down, from head to toe and back again, as though seeing him for the first time. A growing suspicion, a nagging dread, rose from somewhere behind her stomach. "You had handcuffs on you. You took down that man and you handcuffed him. And then… and then you called in someone to take him away." Macey glanced from Trey to Rich to Dana and back to Trey. "You work with them."

Trey hesitated and then nodded once, his gaze never leaving her.

She lifted a hand and held it between them, humiliated to see her fingers shake as so many broken pieces melded together to form a picture she didn't want to see. "You. You said I was clear as of this morning. You said they thought I did these things. That means…that means you thought I did these things."

"Macey." His voice was heavy and jagged with the same anguish her heart felt, cutting her deep into her soul.

"No." She laughed bitterly and backed farther away from him, her hip colliding with the edge of the table. "No. You aren't my friend. You were never my friend. You were lying. All this time you were lying."

Trey opened his mouth to speak, but shut it and threw his hands out to the sides as though he was exasperated and angry.

Emotion slammed Macey in the chest and hammered her heart against the boards. Everything inside her shattered into a million jagged little pieces. She'd trusted him. Liked him. Maybe even…

No. She wouldn't think that.

Two more steps backward to the front door. She had to get out of there. She had to get away from the betrayal, the lies. First Olivia. Now Trey. Nothing was safe. Nothing was true. She had to leave.

She motioned to Kito and turned on her heel. Together, they headed for the door. Macey jerked it open and made a run for the freedom of her own house. The house where Olivia had plotted her demise.

Nowhere was safe.

"Macey!" Trey was on her heels, his hand around her

biceps before she could cross the front porch. "You're in danger. You can't do this. You can't—"

She jerked free and barreled toward her house. Danger came in a lot of forms, and the worst one stood on his front porch, calling her name.

Trey pounded the side of his fist against the door frame as Macey's front door slammed shut. The pain stung all the way up his arm, but he deserved it. He deserved that and a whole lot worse. The look on her face...

He'd broken Macey Price. He'd betrayed her in the same way Olivia had, even if the goal of the deception was very, very different.

Not that it mattered now. She was in danger and needed protection. Racing off to her house alone was foolish. He moved to go after her.

Rich's firm grip on his shoulder stopped him. "Let her go. Give her some time to process. Once she cools off a little bit, Dana can try to talk to her, but you need to stay away. You know that."

Trey wanted to fight, to hit something, to turn around and scream his frustration into Rich's face. Instead, his shoulders slumped. He let his teammate lead him back into the house.

Rich was right. The last thing Macey needed, the last person Macey would ever trust, was Trey. "At least Dana has never lied to her."

"You didn't lie. You did your job. Undercover is tough for a reason. Your other assignments all involved some really bad dudes. This one just happened to be someone you..." Rich opened the front door and walked into the house, then waited for Trey to enter. "Someone you fell for."

Trey faced his teammates. "They should have sent a woman to do this job." A woman wouldn't be in the mess he was in, that was for sure. When it came to his past surveillance subjects, they'd all been hard-core bad operators. Never once had he had to do anything but play the game. With Macey, things had gotten way too real.

He might never recover.

Dana rose from her chair and came to stand next to Rich. "Olivia was savvy. She'd have suspected a woman and would have never let her close. But a man? She never saw you coming."

"Neither did Macey." He waved off any further comments from his friends and forced his mind to shift gears away from his heart. He was an investigator. This was a job. Right now, no matter how much he wanted to simply be a man, that couldn't happen.

Business. He had to be all business. He clapped his hands together. "So, what's next? And how do we keep an eye on Macey when she won't let us near her?" They couldn't force themselves into her home, not without the proper paperwork. Not without an imminent threat outside her door, anyway.

Rich stepped around Trey and headed for the back door. "Right now, I'll take up surveillance of her house. Your deck gives us a clear view of front and back entry points, so we're good there."

"And I'll keep combing through these video files to see what other evidence I can dig up." Dana lifted the tablet from the table and crossed the room to flop into Trey's recliner like someone who was about to binge-watch their favorite TV show. She looked up at Trey. "You take a minute to regroup, and then we need to report back to Captain Harrison what's gone down here since you sent him a cuffed suspect and blew your cover with Macey."

Tough words but true words. Trey didn't like them, and he definitely didn't want to hear them, but Dana was right. He needed to get his head on straight and work the proper channels to move this thing forward and take down the men who were coming after Macey. Right now, they'd proved who the leak was, but so far it didn't get them any closer to the Frye brothers or to Sapphire Skull.

Regroup. Usually, for him, that meant doing something normal. But *normal* had been blown out of the water a long time ago. He wandered into the kitchen and stood between the counter and the refrigerator, feeling like a stranger in his own house. Well, his temporary house, but still.

It was past dinnertime, but Trey wasn't hungry. He grabbed a piece of leftover pizza out of the fridge and forced himself to eat it, then pulled his phone from his hip pocket to report in to the commander.

An unread message flashed on the home screen. His heart beat double time at the sight of Macey's name, and he thumbed the screen to unlock the message.

We've been friends too long to let something stupid make it all awkward. Pretend it never happened?

What was she saying? *Pretend it never happened?* Pretend that he wasn't an undercover investigator and she wasn't in danger? Walk over there to watch the Red Wings play Dallas as though they were two regular people with regular lives? People who had a chance at building something?

If only. For a moment, Trey gripped the phone and stared at the screen. Every iota of the man in him wanted to do exactly that. To buy into the lie that, for one more hockey game, they could be like everybody else.

He poised his thumbs over the screen to ask if she was okay, then caught sight of the time stamp. She'd sent that text a couple of hours ago, minutes before he'd saved her from that horrific attack. She wasn't talking about the wreckage of her life. She was talking about that instant when he'd nearly kissed her.

He shot up a fast prayer of thanks that he hadn't. Kissing her would have made everything so much worse than it already was. Nuclear worse.

With an exhalation that felt like it emptied his lungs, he keyed an I'm sorry, his thumb hovering over the send button. He was sorry, but she'd never believe it. And no investigator would ever say that.

He sent it anyway, then slid the phone into his pocket and jerked the refrigerator open to reach for a soda. He'd go into his office and video call Captain Harrison, explain the evening and see what orders came next. After that?

After that, he had no idea.

Popping the top on the can, he headed for the hallway, but Dana's voice stopped him as he reached his office door. "Um, Trey? We have another problem."

That was more than concern in her voice. It was

genuine alarm. By the time he made it back to the den, she was standing by the recliner, staring at the tablet in her hand. Her jaw was set with a grim look he'd only seen one other time. On her first mission, they'd nearly lost an operative to an assassin who'd figured out they were undercover. Dana's face had looked exactly like that, pinched around the mouth, eyes narrowed, nostrils flared.

Not good. Not good at all.

She walked up the hallway and thrust the tablet at Trey. "Remember the hidden NIC on the laptop? Someone has been using it not only to control the alarm, but to randomly activate the camera. There's a video time-stamped yesterday."

Trey took the tablet, a sick feeling growing in his gut. He stared at the frozen image on the screen. That was a clear shot of him at the laptop, cloning the hard drive, on speakerphone with Dana. He inhaled sharply. "Is there sound?"

Dana reached over and hit the screen.

The video sprang to life.

If Olivia hid something, I can find it. Never underestimate me.

Never said I did.

Trey punched the screen and lifted his eyes to meet Dana's. Someone had been watching the whole time. "They know we know everything."

"And they're probably watching Macey right now."

THIRTEEN

Macey stood in the doorway to Olivia's former bedroom and stared into the darkened space as Kito sat silently beside her in that way he had of knowing she needed him close. Three years. For three years, a traitor to their country had slept in that bed. A criminal. A liar. A backstabbing betrayer who'd manipulated gullible Macey into believing they were friends just so she could set her up and leave her to take the fall.

Didn't they give the death penalty to traitors?

Macey groaned against a nausea so intense she wondered if it might just kill her. She had no idea what her punishment would have been or how close she'd come to being handcuffed and hauled away as a national disgrace.

Handcuffed by her other closest friend.

No, not her closest friend. An agent with the military who'd been pretending from the first time he'd knocked on her door after Kito had jumped the fence into his yard.

They were all pretending. All using her. All caring

more about themselves and their own agendas than they were about her.

Even to the point of throwing her out to the wolves.

Macey slipped into the room slowly, half-afraid a killer would rise from the shadows wielding a knife or a box cutter. She made her way on tiptoe to the window, a stranger in her own house. Slipping one slat of the blinds up, she peeked at Trey's backyard, which sat at an angle to her own.

In the dim light from his kitchen window, a man sat on Trey's porch, facing her house. It was too bulky of a dude to be Trey. Probably Rich, keeping an eye on things.

That was either terrifying or comforting.

Having her house watched was invasive, but what else could she do? Call the police? Hire private bodyguards? How would she even find someone like that?

There was nowhere to go. She couldn't try to hide at her mom's and risk raining danger on her head, though her mother would relish the excitement, at least for a little while. Every spy movie she'd ever watched said her car was probably being tracked. Maybe she could take a ride-share to the airport, but she had no idea how to go into hiding in a way that was foolproof or feasible.

She didn't even know who she was running from.

She had no choice but to allow Trey and his friends to stand guard, even if the pain of his actions cut almost as deep as Olivia's. Regardless of any deception Trey had perpetrated, he'd had a good reason.

That reason involved men who were willing to torture her to get information she couldn't give them. Information she wouldn't give them, even if she knew where it was. Somehow, Olivia had made everyone believe she was the thief all along. Then she'd died and left Macey to burn up in the fallout.

Kito rose from his spot at her feet and trotted into the living room. Knowing him, he could feel the vibes of her tension and had had enough for one night.

She sank to the edge of Olivia's bed, staring at a photo on the bookcase of the two of them at Carowinds. Olivia had been scared to ride the Carolina Cyclone. Macey had pushed her until she would. They'd both laughed afterward at Olivia's terror, then gorged on ice cream and corn dogs.

It had all been a lie.

A noise from the living room brought her to her feet, heart hammering. Why didn't she own a gun? At this point, even her self-defense skills had failed her. She backed against the wall at the sound of the front door opening and Kito's toenails tapping on the hardwood, heading for a new friend. A new friend who was probably out to—

"Macey!" Trey's voice, frantic and harsh, bounced into the room.

She froze before all of the anger and bitterness rushed in and set her feet into motion. Macey stalked across the room and down the short hallway, where she confronted Trey as he strode across the living room toward her. "Did you ask to come into my house? Do you have any kind of warrant? Any kind of—"

He edged past her and down the hall to the bedroom she used as a guest room and office, where he strode to the bookcase in the corner.

"What are you doing? You can't go through my stuff

without permission." She wanted to shove him in the back, to hit him and make him stop, but that wasn't her nature. Instead, her voice grew shrill and loud. "I'm innocent, remember?"

He ignored her. Instead, he reached up and pulled the internet modem from the top shelf. For a moment, he held the device in his hands and stared at it. Then he ripped the plug out. He dropped the box to the floor and smashed it beneath his foot.

Macey shrieked, then buried her fist against her lips. Plastic shards flew toward her and skittered along the floor past her feet. What was he doing?

When Trey turned, the outline of a holstered pistol showed at his hip.

Somehow, the knowledge that he was armed brought her situation into stark reality. Everything was completely out of control.

Macey opened her fist and covered her mouth, her breath warm on her fingers. She couldn't speak. Couldn't react. Couldn't do anything at all except stare at this man she knew so well who was now nothing more than a stranger. A man who acted out of character, who carried a weapon...

He slipped past her into the hall and went to the bar near the kitchen, where he stared up at the wall, scanning the area as though he planned to remodel her house or measure for pictures.

When Macey caught her breath, she dared to step closer to him, stopping between the hallway and his position. If he was into smashing things randomly, there was no way to know what he'd do next. The change in him threw her off-kilter, rocked her in another nauseating direction. "What are you doing?" The words came on a whisper.

"Somebody's been watching you. Has been watching both of us." His voice was heavy and resigned. Without looking away from the sensor on the wall between the kitchen and the living room, he motioned her closer.

Caught between truth and lies, trust and betrayal, Macey hesitated. He could do anything. Handcuff her. Shove her in a closet. How could she be sure he was one of the good guys?

Because he was Trey. Deep inside, something in her knew he wouldn't hurt her, even if he'd been lying to her for months. He might not be the guy who would stay, but he was the guy who'd protect her until he left for something better.

She chose to believe that and eased closer until she stood only a couple of feet away from him. "What are we looking at?"

He pointed at the motion sensor. "I'm ninety-nine-percent certain that's a camera. Follow me." Walking into the living room, he studied the wall behind the couch, then pointed to another sensor. "That's one, too. Based on what Dana has found, there's one in the garage and one in the hallway, too."

"Bedrooms?" The word choked out, barely audible. She felt violated, robbed of all security. Ready to flee the home that was rapidly becoming a house of horrors.

"Only public spaces." Trey kicked at the carpet, then turned toward Macey. "At least Olivia had *some* common decency in her." Absentmindedly, he petted Kito's head when the dog trotted up. He gave the husky a quick side pat, then pointed to his bed in the corner of the living room.

Kito padded away and lay down.

"The laptop that controlled the alarm had a hidden wireless card on it. It's been hooked up to the outside world the entire time. Anytime you opened it, it transferred data to another computer somewhere, including whatever it downloaded from the cameras. It could be accessed even when it was closed. The only way to stop the surveillance for certain was to destroy the modem." His eyebrow tracked toward his hairline and he looked like a guilty little boy. "Sorry for the drama." He glanced at his watch and slipped back into his government persona. "I need you to pack a bag with some clothes. No phone, no electronics. We have to get out of here. They know we're investigating. They could show up at—"

"I need a minute." Macey held up a hand, rounded the couch and sank onto the edge of the coffee table. Information overload had robbed her brain of logical thought. Wireless cards and cameras, and being watched in her own home? She was going to be sick. She pulled in huge breaths and tried to regain some sort of control before she fell apart completely. "You at least owe me some answers before I trust you to drag me off into the dark of night."

After a short hesitation, Trey followed her footsteps and sat beside her, his shoulder almost touching hers.

Smart man to keep a little bit of distance. "I'm still not sure how I feel about you. For months, you've lied to me."

"I know."

"I'm pretty sure I'm angry that you'd think I could be such a horrible person. That you could lie to me about…about everything." She sniffed at the sudden sting of tears. He didn't get to see her cry. He had lost the right to comfort her.

But the truth was, *his* betrayal was only the icing on a very bitter cake. "Honestly, what Olivia did hurts worse."

"I know that, too."

She ventured a sideways glance at him. His elbows rested on his knees, his hands clasped between them. He was staring at the floor. That profile was ridiculously familiar from countless hours of watching hockey, and frankly, it was comforting.

Macey sighed. "Was anything about you real?"

He chewed the inside of his lower lip. "My last name isn't Burns. I'm not from Toledo. I'm not a staff sergeant in an infantry unit." Trey stared at the floor for a long moment before he turned his head and caught her gaze. "My wife really left me exactly the way I told you. My best friend really died in a drag race gone wrong. I really was almost killed, too. Jesus really did change my life. And at some point, Macey…" He turned to look at the couch and shook his head. "At some point everything between us became all too real."

"Even this morning." Her voice was low, barely a whisper. If he said no, she couldn't bear it.

"Even this morning." The words were raw and heavy, ragged with something she couldn't comprehend, even though her heart picked up a rhythm it definitely should not have. "I shouldn't have let it get real. That goes against everything I'm trained to do. But once I suspected you were innocent, nothing in me was willing to hold back, no matter how hard I tried."

"You only found out I was innocent this morning."

"I've known pretty much since I started investigating you. I just didn't have proof." He turned and looked her in the eye so suddenly that she didn't have a chance to look away. "You're not the type. There's not an evil bone in you. Not like Olivia. I started trying to prove the evidence was wrong. I was probably biased, which means I'm a terrible investigator." He braced his hands on his knees and stood, pacing away from her.

There was nothing to do but watch him. What could she do with a man who claimed he was her friend, who acted as though he was attracted to her, but who couldn't act on it? And what could she do while standing in the doorway between life and death while men who were well versed in torture waited to snatch her away?

"I'm still being a terrible investigator." Trey glanced at his watch. "Pack your clothes. Put them in a garbage bag in case someone has tagged your suitcases. Grab your ID but nothing else in your wallet. We have to leave in the next ten minutes. We're already pushing it. They may not have seen me make that arrest tonight but they definitely saw me on the cameras. They know I'm investigating them. My cover's blown wide-open, which means they're going to do something big soon to keep me from getting you to safety. Go. Before they make good on their threats to destroy you."

Trey texted Rich to pack up, also letting him know they were about to move. Then he paced the living room while Macey pulled out drawers and rummaged through her closet. Letting her out of his sight even to pack tore at his nerves, but he didn't want to alarm her any more than he had to. Olivia might be dead, but it was clear from the access records Dana had found that someone else was keeping tabs on the house. Someone who continued to believe that Macey was the source of their pirated information. That she'd taken their money and was about to run.

With all he had inside him, he prayed for time. He'd grown so hyperfocused on proving that Macey was innocent, he'd dropped every ball out there on searching for who was coming after her. He'd been on defense instead of offense, and now it was too late. They were on the run, which made everything worse.

A soft sound on the far side of the living room lifted his head. Macey stood at the entrance to the short hallway that led to her bedroom. She held a lumpy white kitchen garbage bag and looked like a lost child. "Kito?"

At his name, the dog lifted his head but remained on his cushion, where Trey had banished him earlier. He might be a headstrong pup, but he was an obedient one when his stubborn streak took a break.

No way could they leave him behind. In their quest to make Macey talk, those killers might even go after her beloved companion to cause her pain. "Where's his leash?"

"Hanging on the hook just inside the garage door."

Trey grabbed it and clapped his hands together, Kito's signal to come. The dog jumped up, his whole body wriggling as he leaped repeatedly at the sight of his leash. Trey leaned over and clipped the latch to the ring on his collar. "Sorry it's not a real *w-a-l-k*, buddy," Trey muttered. "But you do get to go for a ride in my truck, so that should console you a little." A long ride. They were headed to the home of Captain Gavin Harrison's army buddy just outside Mountain Springs, about five hours' drive.

It was going to be a long night.

"Ready?"

Macey didn't move. Instead she stood, gripping the bag so tightly that her knuckles were nearly white. "No. I need…" She pulled in a deep breath and looked straight into his eyes. "This isn't some weekend trip. This could be a really long time. I may never have my life back. This is all too fast."

"Now that we're on their trail, Dana and the team can start tracing them from their connection to your house. It might not be that long before we end this."

"Stop. You're talking about a whole ring of criminals. I know their reach is long. I know nowhere is really safe."

Dropping Kito's leash, Trey gave up pretending he could keep his distance. Macey was in pain and he needed to help her. He crossed the room and pulled her to him before he thought the whole action through. He wanted to hold her close, to shield and protect her and to promise her he could keep her safe.

But he couldn't, and she shoved him away.

"You're part of the problem. I'm trusting you because I have no other choice." She pulled the bag up in front of her and hugged it to her chest. "Right now it seems like everything is a lie. Like everyone is letting me down. Like there's no one stable."

Now wasn't the time to try to convince her that he was going to stick by her and that God was, too. Now wasn't the time for anything except ushering her to his truck and getting on the road before some faceless monster made another move against her. "We need to talk about this while we're moving. I know you need time. I get that. But we don't have—"

A loud pop and a crash at the front door stopped his sentence cold. Trey whirled, stepping between Macey and the door as he reached for his weapon.

But there was no time to draw.

Two men burst through the door. One leveled a pistol on Trey and the other held a small Skorpion machine gun.

Macey screamed but bit it off halfway. Trey could feel her standing tall behind him as though she refused to cower before men who were determined to terrorize her.

Good for her. He needed her to be strong right now. The only reason these two thugs hadn't fired and taken him down was likely that they were wary of hitting Macey, who they still believed had the intelligence they wanted. She was safe from death and, as long as he was near her, so was he. But if they were separated or if those thugs took Macey away...

Then he was as good as dead, and she would suffer torture that nauseated him even in his imagination.

"Step away from her. She's ours." The pistol-toting thug circled to Trey's left, cutting off the escape route to the back door while the second gunman maintained his position near the front door.

It was possible Macey and Trey could slip around

the corner and through the kitchen to the garage, but they'd get no farther. It would take too long for the garage door to lift for them to duck under it. Thug Two would be out the front door waiting for them before they could escape.

They were trapped.

But he wasn't handing over Macey. They'd have to go through him to get to her.

If only he hadn't told Rich to stand down…

Wait. If he could get these two talking, could stall them long enough, then eventually Rich and Dana would figure out something was wrong and head this way. Hopefully with weapons at the ready.

"Move now." The guy's drawl was familiar. Trey hadn't gotten a good look at the two who'd come after Macey on that first night, but the voice was one he'd never forget.

"You failed to get her the first two times, so now you're trying again?" Trey moved his hand from his side, praying his shirt covered the pistol at his hip. If they didn't know he had it, he could maintain the element of surprise. "I'm sure whoever your boss is isn't happy that you came back empty-handed the last time." Trey pretended to think. He was goading them, but that was good. Angry men were rarely men who were thinking, and if he could keep them off balance, he could eventually outsmart them. "Oh wait. You didn't leave empty-handed. You left with a worthless picture. Of your boss, I'm guessing?"

The man by the door eased closer. His face drawn tight.

His buddy with the pistol twisted his lip. His nose

twitched slightly, almost as though he was losing his composure. "I'm not telling you again to move."

This was the tightrope Trey now walked. Keep them angry enough to make a misstep but not angry enough to fire at will.

"You hand her over and we leave you alive. Or better yet, she hands over what she has and we leave you both alive. We all walk away from this in one piece." The man raised his pistol and leveled it, though his hand and voice both shook slightly with barely sheathed anger. "Otherwise, you die, we take her, and we make her talk."

"Do you think I'm dumb enough to fall for that? If I move, you shoot me, then you take her."

The man jerked the pistol higher.

Macey jumped and bumped into Trey's back. "What if I come with you? Myself? And I take you to the intel? What will that buy me? My freedom? His life?"

The pistol lowered an inch. "You have what we want?"

"I do."

Trey's heart sank to his knees, making them so heavy they nearly dropped him to the floor. Had she been lying to him all along?

He'd been fooled again. He'd let a woman turn his head, let himself believe that he...that he loved her. That maybe she also loved him. Despite the danger, he ached to turn and unleash his hurt, his anger, his betrayal. He wanted to—

"Will you promise not to hurt him?" Macey's voice was strong, with an accent not her own.

Could it be she'd changed that much? That she'd been

so deep into her con of him that she'd changed everything about herself?

The man with the pistol stepped closer, until he was
just out of Trey's reach. "We won't hurt him if you come
with me."

They'd kill him no matter what they promised her.
She had to know that.

Macey rested her hand between his shoulder blades
and let it slide toward his right side. She knew his pistol was there. She wouldn't disarm him, would she?

"If we surrender and I return with you, will you
promise not to hurt this man?" There was that odd ca-
dence, that out-of-place accent again. It tweaked at a
memory this time.

The thug's head cocked to one side. He'd already
answered her once.

What was Macey doing?

Trey froze. Those words. That tone. There was something familiar about them both. Something that lifted
his spirit. That spoke to his heart. That reminded him
of—

Of that movie. The one she'd made him watch over
and over. That princess movie she could quote word for
word. She was quoting it now, the scene where Butter-
cup agreed to surrender in exchange for Westley's freedom. It was a signal the bad guys wouldn't pick up.

She wasn't turning on him. She was working to save
them. The line before the one she was quoting popped
out of his mouth. "Death first."

He heard Macey's exhalation and knew she under-
stood.

He was telling her to move forward with her plan.

He just prayed she was a good enough shot to immobilize both men before they figured out what she was doing. And he prayed he was right, and that she wasn't about to betray him straight into death.

As her fingers slid to his holster and closed around the pistol, Trey knew this was it. They were either about to survive or they were about to die. Together.

FOURTEEN

He'd heard her. He knew what she was doing. Macey nearly sagged in relief, something she'd once thought only happened in movies.

When he'd tensed at her initial declaration, she'd nearly abandoned the plan, knowing it had to feel like a knife digging into his back.

Then she'd figured out how to tell him.

And he'd heard.

She'd never loved him more than she did in that moment. Because she did love him, and she was going to do whatever it took to save him.

Macey's fingers closed around the unfamiliar grip of Trey's pistol as he angled his right side toward her. She slipped the weapon from its holster, took one step back from Trey as though she was about to step around him and prayed to the God she was beginning to believe in. With a deep breath, she steadied herself. "Now!"

Trey dropped to one knee and Macey fired.

The man closest to them cried out and dropped his pistol, gripping his shoulder.

Before Macey could register what was happening,

Trey lunged for the loose pistol and came up on one knee, firing a round at the man near the front door.

Rather than fire back, Thug Two turned and bolted into the night. A shout from the front yard followed his escape.

Macey froze, the weapon gripped in her hands and her arms outstretched. Had she really just fired a gun? At a human being? Had she taken a life?

The shaking started as Dana ran into the house with her pistol drawn. She holstered the weapon and slid to her knees next to the man Macey had shot. "Trey, get Macey."

In the next instant, he was beside her, his hand resting near her wrist. "It's okay, Mace. You can lower the weapon. I'll take it. You did good."

Macey allowed Trey to ease the gun from her fingers and reholster it. He pulled her to him.

She sank against him as a quaking came from deep inside her. She was cold. She was hot. She was coming apart. Armed men. In her house. And she'd shot one.

Trey pulled her head to his shoulder and spoke past her ear. "You have him?"

"Yeah. Rich tackled the one running out of the house. We figured something was wrong when you guys didn't show. Rich spotted these guys through the window and called for backup. They'll haul our friends here away shortly."

Trey nodded, then turned his full attention to Macey. "You're safe. You did good."

"I shot a man." She whispered the words harshly into his shoulder. "Did I kill him?" With everything in her, she hoped not. In all that had happened, taking another life would destroy her.

"He won't use his shoulder for a while, but he'll live to stand trial."

She nodded, then took a deep breath and pulled herself together. She couldn't fall apart. No matter what Trey said, she wasn't safe. If they were going to hide, then Trey couldn't stop to pick her up and carry her when her limbs turned to water. "Can you get me out of here? To where..." She glanced at the man on the floor, who could still hear her. "To somewhere else?"

"I've got this." Dana's voice broke in between them.

Trey laid his hands on Macey's shoulders and searched her face. "Are you sure?"

"Where's Kito?" Please don't let her have shot her dog. She ripped away from Trey and glanced around the room. "Kito!"

"He's fine." Trey pressed a kiss to her forehead, then gently turned her toward her bedroom.

Kito peeked around the door, then trotted up the short hallway and leaned against Macey's leg. She dropped to her knees and pressed her forehead to his, closing her eyes. Why couldn't she go back a week to when Kito only had to comfort her when she was sad about her best friend's death? When Trey was her friend and not a military investigator? Before killers and lies and secrets invaded her life in a way that surely didn't happen in the real world?

Normal was a craving she couldn't fight.

"Macey?" Trey squatted beside her and laid a hand on her back. "We need to go."

They were the four heaviest words she'd ever heard.

When she walked out that front door, there was no guarantee she'd ever come back.

But she pulled herself together one more time, grasped Kito's leash and allowed Trey to help her up from her knees. She had to. There wasn't a choice if she wanted to live.

Somehow she made it to the truck, got Kito settled and her seat belt buckled, and held it together as Trey pulled out of the neighborhood and headed for I-95, watching the rearview as much as he watched out the windshield. He probably hoped she wouldn't notice but she did.

She noticed too many things. The kick of the pistol in her hand. The smell of gunpowder. The look on that man's face when the bullet found its mark.

"You okay?" Trey's voice was low in the darkened truck, and his hand found hers where it rested on the seat. He wrapped his fingers around hers.

Something else she remembered… The sound of Trey's voice when she'd told those men she had what they wanted, when she'd taken the risk that she could save them both.

She sniffed. "You thought I betrayed you. That I'd been lying to you the whole time."

"For a minute, yes." His fingers tightened on hers. "You were pretty convincing."

Macey nodded and turned her head to stare at the darkness outside her window. He didn't try to deny it or talk around it. Somehow, his honesty took away some of the sting. It felt like he respected her enough to tell her the truth, even when it was hard to hear. A small part of her heart that had backed away when she'd found out who he truly was edged in his direction.

"You have to understand where I come from."

"I do." His ex-wife's abandonment was too much like her mother's behavior. Self-centered and selfish. They'd both been deeply wounded and scarred by those who were supposed to care the most. "And I don't blame you." She pulled her hand from his and balled her fist on her thigh. Even though he'd earned back her trust, she wasn't sure what to think, what was real with him and what wasn't. He'd held her hand, pulled her close, kissed her on the forehead... But was that real? Was he still playing a game? Was it how he'd comfort any woman?

Surely not. But still, she was falling fast for him. The larger question was how he felt about her. And how she'd ever feel free to be in a relationship. "After what we've both been through, after all of the lies and the hurt, how do we ever trust anyone again?"

In the dim glow from the dashboard lights, Trey winced. He gripped the steering wheel with both hands and negotiated the on-ramp to the highway. "That's why it's called *trust*. Otherwise, it would be *certainty* or *knowing*, I guess."

Made sense, but it didn't help.

Trey watched the road. "Here's the truth, and you're not going to like it even though it's probably something you already know."

His words were heavy. Macey reached to the floorboard behind her and rubbed Kito's head where he'd curled up between the front and back seats.

"Every human being alive will fail you. They'll hurt

you. It's inevitable. Even if they don't want to, it's going to happen. You know that well. And, Macey, you've hurt people, too."

This was personal. Macey wanted to argue that she had never deliberately lied to anyone or set them up to go to prison for horrific crimes, but she couldn't seem to get her emotions worked up. She was too tired. Exhausted beyond reason.

"It doesn't have to be big hurts, Mace. Even smaller wrongs can leave lasting impressions."

She pressed her fist harder against her thigh. He was right. She didn't want him to be, but he was. "So there's nowhere safe. Nowhere to truly put your faith." She'd always known it. But now, even as she spoke, she knew what he was going to say next. Something deep inside her was ready to hear it. Craved to hear it. "You're going to say God."

He chuckled softly. "Sounds to me like you already know."

"Maybe. But I don't know how to trust what I can't see. I don't know how to trust a God that does things His way. Like, my mother still chooses herself over anyone else. You still wrecked. Your ex-wife still left you."

"True, but God has used those things in my life. When you trust Him, He'll use yours, too. The bad doesn't go to waste. Because of Gia, I have a deeper understanding of what people who have been betrayed like you've been betrayed feel. I've been able to walk beside friends who have been hurt. And because of that wreck… Well, God moved me into this job, where I've stopped things from happening in this country that you'd never imagine. I've brought bad guys to justice."

He tapped the steering wheel with his thumb. "I'm here with you right now."

"You're here because you were trying to prove I was selling secrets to our enemies. Because you thought I was a criminal." The truth stung all over again.

Yellow lines disappeared under the front of the truck for several miles before Trey spoke. "I doubt Olivia expected you would be in danger from the men she betrayed, but she did make you look guilty to anyone with eyes to see." He held up a hand to stop her from speaking, then dropped it back to the steering wheel. "You were going to be investigated because of her setup. It was inevitable. If it hadn't been me, it would have been someone else. Someone who might not have recognized your innocence in time to save you." His words were low, but she felt the weight of them.

If Trey hadn't truly gotten to know her... If it had been someone else looking for evidence... Then they might have pronounced her guilty. This wasn't about Trey and her feelings for him. This was about the right person being set into place to recognize her innocence and to rescue her from a life of imprisonment and ostracism.

"God did that." Her whispered words barely penetrated the air in the truck, but somehow Trey heard them.

His hand slipped from the steering wheel and found hers again, lifting her fist from her leg and uncurling her fingers until he had her safely in his grasp. "He did. The situation isn't humanly perfect. Our situations on earth will never be humanly perfect, because we live in a world that's a mess. But God can take a messed-up thing and make it perfect. He did it for you in this situation." Trey held on to her hand tighter, as though he could squeeze his words up her arm and into her soul. "He wants to do that for your whole life." He laughed softly. "I sound like a preacher, but it's true. I don't know a better way to say it, but He wants to fix what's wrong inside you and make you right with Him."

"Like you are."

"Like I am. My life's not perfect, but it's so much better with God. Even when it all falls apart, I can trust He's got something in the works to make it worthwhile in the end. Something He can use for good down the line. It's something you can trust, even when you can't see."

Macey clung to Trey's hand, trying to grasp what he was saying. It was right there. Right in front of her. But somehow, in this dark truck, fleeing for her very life, she couldn't seem to grab it and hold on.

Pink and orange light tinged the edges of the mountains. Trey turned off the road and pulled onto the dirt lane that wound up the side of a mountain to Arch Thompson's house. The family home of Captain Harrison's "battle buddy," it was a huge plot of land that sprawled most of the way down into the valley. A tree-filled oasis, it was the perfect tucked-away hiding place for a woman on the run.

And for the man who was falling for her.

Trey lifted his foot from the accelerator and coasted to a stop on the winding drive. He glanced at Macey, who'd fallen asleep a couple of hours earlier, her head against the headrest and one hand between the seats on Kito's neck.

There was no denying it. Something was happening between them, something big. He was drawn to the way she outshouted him during hockey games. The way she stood up against the fiercest adversity he'd ever seen another human being face. The way she treated the dog who hadn't started out as hers, but who had become another piece of her heart.

And there was nothing he could do about it, because there was no telling where she'd be tomorrow.

As Rich's truck rolled into view behind him, Trey eased his truck back into motion. The engine revved higher as the grade grew steeper.

Rich kept his distance, just in case Trey didn't give the accelerator enough gas.

Macey sniffed and stirred. She stretched her arms over her head, then glanced around as though she wasn't sure where she was. When she spotted Trey, her forehead wrinkled in a way he'd call cute under other circumstances. Then her eyes focused and she set her face toward the windshield.

Trey turned his attention to the lane in front of him. "Sleep well?"

"I guess."

"You were out for a while. At least since before Hickory. I think everything finally caught up to you. I know when I was overseas, I got to where I could sleep anywhere, even standing up."

"How about we don't let it get that far." She stretched again and petted Kito's head when he stuck his nose between the seats and rested his chin on the center console. "The sky's pretty."

Trey looked up from the road and let the truck ease

to a stop again. Rich would understand why and had probably already stopped anyway.

To their right, the mountain dropped away about twenty feet from the vehicle and opened up the view of a broad valley. Wispy morning clouds blazed like flames across the sky, set afire by the sun that wasn't yet visible over the mountains. It was a sunrise that rivaled the most beautiful he'd ever seen. Part of him wanted to take Macey's hand and just sit, to share a beautiful moment together. His hand dropped from the steering wheel and inched toward hers.

Macey was intent on the view. "It's like that saying, 'Red sky at night, sailor's delight. Red sky at morning…'"

"'Sailor take warning.'" Trey finished the adage with her and withdrew his hand. For a moment, he'd forgotten this was a mission and Macey was fleeing for her life.

Suddenly, the crimson sky wasn't beautiful. It was an ominous reminder of the danger that stalked them.

He glanced in the rearview. Rich had stopped about thirty feet behind him, and both he and Dana had their faces turned to the sunrise. If only he and Macey could have had that. Now that Dana worked with Rich and was out of the WitSec game, they were planning a future.

WitSec. Trey gripped the steering wheel and eased onto the accelerator for the last short climb to the Thompson house. It was possible Macey could be whisked away from him into hiding soon. She'd been his mission for so long—first to investigate and now to protect—that it had never occurred to him she could become someone else's responsibility.

Yeah, that sunrise was a warning, all right. In more ways than one.

When he pulled up to the sprawling two-story white farmhouse, his commander's truck was already sitting to the right of the three-car garage built to resemble an old pole barn. Captain Harrison stepped out of the house, holding a coffee mug, and pointed to the center and right garage bays, which already stood open.

So they weren't even taking chances with his truck being out in the open way up here. This was full hiding. Some would say the captain was overly cautious, but as a former SF soldier and police chief, he was the smartest and most tactically cunning man Trey had ever met. He'd trust Gavin Harrison with his life and had done so more than once.

As soon as they parked, Macey slid from the truck, opened the rear door and grabbed Kito's leash. "Where can I walk him?"

"You can take him to the side of the garage. Just don't wander too far." Captain Harrison appeared in the garage doorway as Rich pulled into the middle bay.

Macey nodded and stepped into the fresh morning sunlight. In the light, she looked different somehow. Tired and stressed, but there was something else, some sort of something that exuded the kind of calm she hadn't managed to achieve earlier when she'd been fighting to hold herself in check. Maybe she'd rested better than he'd thought.

Captain Harrison watched Macey round the corner and waited for Rich and Dana to join them. "We don't have a counselor on the team, but I've got a call in to Amy. She's got experience with this stuff. It might be good for Macey to have a chat with her. Soon as y'all give me the go-ahead, she'll come up and be an ear for her."

"Smart." Rich stretched his arms above his head and leaned back, a motion Trey mimicked. The drive had been long and nerve-racking, even after Rich and Dana had pulled in behind him to provide rear cover. "Amy's probably a good idea." Rich turned to Trey and lowered his arms. "You good with that?"

Trey didn't know Amy Maldonado well, but he'd heard stories. Dana had been a part of the team protecting Amy from human traffickers who'd wanted her dead.

Dana elbowed Trey in the ribs. "Might not be such a bad idea for you to talk to Sam, too."

Sam. Amy's husband, who had fallen in love with her while protecting her. He'd definitely understand how Trey was feeling, but Sam couldn't do anything else in their current situation.

Trey wanted to elbow her back but he refrained. As far as he knew, the commander was in the dark about Trey's feelings for Macey. He'd like to keep it that way until he could tell him on his own.

Unfortunately, the way Captain Harrison watched him as he took a sip of coffee said he already knew.

"You going to keep drinking that coffee in front of us or are you planning to offer us all about a gallon of the stuff." Rich didn't wait for an answer but brushed past Captain Harrison and headed for the house. "Some of us have been up for over twenty-four hours."

"Some of you need to stop being heroes." The commander turned and followed Rich and Dana, but not before a quick glance behind Trey and a raised eyebrow.

When Trey turned, Macey was walking back with Kito on his leash. The dog bounded and pulled in every direction, keyed up and wriggling over the multitude of squirrels and birds that chattered and chirped in the woods surrounding them.

Jerking the leash to rein him in, Macey flashed Trey a quick smile. "He's in husky paradise. If I let him off this leash, he'll terrorize the squirrels until he either catches one or drops from exhaustion."

Trey actually found himself laughing. Kito was legendary for his squirrel hunting. He'd never managed to actually catch one, but the dog's hope sprang eternal.

"Good thing he's into chasing them or I might have been home the night that…" Macey trailed off and sank to Trey's bumper, wrapping Kito's leash around her hand. She stared at the large white farmhouse that had been in the Thompson family for generations. "I was so mad at him that night for taking off. I couldn't figure out how he'd gotten out of the house, but I'm guessing he bolted when those men opened the door. If he'd stayed inside or run in a different direction instead of past me, I'd have probably walked right in on them. They'd have disappeared with me before you'd ever gotten home."

"Or if I'd gotten the call five minutes later…" Trey sat beside her on the bumper, his shoulder brushing hers. It was enough.

With his trademark doggy sigh, Kito dropped to the ground at their feet, panting from the exertion of trying to get those squirrels.

"I guess that's more of what you were talking about earlier, how God is in control even when we don't see it. He didn't keep all of this from happening to me, but He's made a way through it. I thought a lot about that on the ride last night before I fell asleep." Macey rubbed the toe of her Converse lightly along Kito's belly. "I thought about a lot of things."

Trey's heart picked up the pace. He'd never been the type to talk about salvation a lot, although he'd had some intensely personal Jesus conversations with others.

"I did some praying, too." Macey stopped petting the dog.

Trey's head snapped up and his eyes locked on hers. "You did?" He tried to keep his voice level, but it cracked in a way he'd normally find embarrassing.

Macey smiled softly. Clearly, she'd heard his flashback to puberty. "Since He's so good at taking control, I decided to let Him have it. All of it." This time, she reached for Trey's hand instead of the other way around, and the feeling ran up his arm in a way no other touch ever had. "I don't know how this is going to end, but He does. And in some strange way I can't explain, I'm okay with Him knowing. I'm not okay with the situation, but I'm okay with Him being in charge of it. And I have to trust that He's nothing like my mother. He won't take off when the excitement is over."

"He won't."

"And neither will you."

This was a feeling Trey had never felt before. Something in him shifted. The emotions that had been growing changed into something deeper, rarer. It was something he'd never felt with any other woman, not even Gia. There was no way to explain it. It was peace. It was joy. It was a calm spot in the midst of this storm that battered them both.

Macey felt it, too. It was in her expression, something undefinable. That sense of calm he'd noticed when she'd climbed out of the truck earlier.

In some way, it was a new freedom that defied explanation, but one that settled in his heart with the same kind of certainty he'd had when he'd prayed about taking the assignment with Overwatch.

This was true. This was right. This was exactly where he should be.

He planted his foot and angled toward Macey, watching her eyes to see if her thoughts ran parallel to his. Something told him they did, but he needed to be sure.

She dipped her chin, then lifted it, holding his gaze in a way that let him know that, yes, she'd felt that atomic explosion in her emotions, as well.

Every other time he'd ever wanted to kiss a woman, it had been physical attraction drawing him. This time, it was more. If he kissed Macey, it would change both of their lives forever.

And he was ready.

FIFTEEN

Macey met Trey halfway. This wasn't something she'd planned. When she'd sat and he'd settled beside her, she'd only meant to tell him she was different from how she had been when they'd fled her home. She had given over her life to the control of Someone larger than herself, to the One that Trey trusted.

But when she'd said that, it was like a door had opened between her and Trey. Like God had somehow given her permission to feel again.

Not *permission* to. The *ability* to.

As his lips met hers, she gripped Kito's leash and Trey's hand tighter. If she could hold on to this feeling forever, she would. In the midst of a storm, this was peace. This was joy. This was a sense of wholeness she'd never felt before. Not in her job. Not in her family. Somehow this was a gift from God that she never wanted to give back.

But it couldn't last.

When Trey pulled away, Macey let him go. She had no other choice.

He stayed a breath away from her, and she could

feel his reluctance as much as she could feel her own. Finally, he stood. "We can't."

Pressing his lips together, he turned his face to the sky. "We can't do this. An hour from now, you could be under someone else's protection. For now, you're safe here. I'm guessing the commander would be okay with you having the run of the place as long as you stay in sight of the house. Arch Thompson isn't here, but he's got several acres, fenced well enough for even Kito to roam without getting into too much trouble. But I don't know how long my chain of command will let you stay here. They'll most likely insist you go into some sort of protective custody."

And she'd stay there until every single unknown person who was chasing her was caught. "I might never see you again." The pain sliced her heart. Why? Why would God let her find Trey only to snatch her away from him? She was too new at reading God's mind. And she was afraid of what she'd find there if she could.

She looked up at the house and let her gaze wander the unfamiliar property. This wasn't a place of peace. It was a place of necessity. A place of hiding. It wasn't Trey and her on a romantic sunrise date. Inside that house, three people were strategizing a way to protect her and to take down a group of dangerous men and women.

Kito seemed to sense her tension once again and he rose to rest his chin on her knee. She buried her fingers in his neck fur. "What happens now?"

Trey watched the door through which the rest of his team had vanished. His forehead furrowed. "I'm not sure. I was pretty much in charge up until my cover was blown. Now it all goes higher than me. Probably even higher than Captain Harrison. There are decisions to be made."

A door creaked and both of them turned toward the house. From the porch, Trey's commander waved him over. Far from the welcoming look he'd worn a few moments earlier, his expression was now tight and concerned.

Macey might have found her peace with God but, in her situation, a little bit of fear was warranted. It washed over her like a boiling wave. Whatever that expression on the commander's face was, it was about her, and it wasn't good.

Trey swept out his hand for her to lead the way to the house, but Macey tightened her grip on Kito's leash and shook her head. She couldn't do it. She couldn't face going inside. Out here, in the fresh morning sunlight, the slightly chilled air and the scent of trees, there was a sense of peace, of a closeness with the God she was only beginning to recognize. Indoors was…

Well, in her mind it was dark and closed off and stale. If things went the way she suspected and Trey had hinted, indoors with the blinds closed was going to be her life for the foreseeable future. She was going to soak up every small freedom while she could. "Can I stay out here? I'll stay in sight of the back of the house, like y'all asked. I just can't face being cooped up right now. It feels like prison." A shudder hit her stomach at the word. *Prison* was exactly where she would have landed if it hadn't been for Trey's belief in her innocence.

Trey glanced at the house. "Stay in sight. If I look

out and don't see you…" He pointed toward a large bay window to the left of the back door, but his expression said it all. Even a man like Trey, fearless to the core, had his concerns. "I'll be right by that window."

His fear scared her more than anything, if she was being honest.

He jogged to the house as Macey sank onto the truck's bumper, holding Kito's leash loosely in her hand. Everything in her life was moving a thousand miles an hour. When she pumped the brakes, all she got was a pedal that hit the floor without slowing her speed.

Kito rose from his position at her feet and rested his chin on her knee.

"You're my good boy, aren't you?" Macey patted his head, then ran both hands around his neck, scratching beneath his collar. It was bound to be uncomfortable, but there was no way she was taking the leash off. Those squirrels would have him twelve miles away before she could even register he was gone. If she lost Kito now, it might be the single thing that finally devastated her.

Bending low, she rested her forehead against his and exhaled. It might have been Olivia who'd brought Kito home, but the dog had definitely become Macey's.

She shut her eyes. It was probably the one good, true gift Olivia had given to her.

A soft sound from the corner of the garage pricked Kito's ears. He pulled away from Macey and faced the area where Macey had taken him when they first arrived.

Macey stood and let Kito lead her to the corner. He pranced the way he always did when he needed a little bit of relief. "Didn't finish the first time, did you?" Ruffling his neck fur, Macey unraveled the leash from around her wrist and held on to the loop at the end, letting him lead the way.

She glanced back at the house. If Trey happened to look, he'd guess where she was, knowing she'd already had to haul Kito around the barn once before. It would only be a second anyway. He'd never even know she was gone.

They rounded the corner and Kito paused at a bush in the landscaping along the side of the barn. While he did, Macey turned to catch the view, which was truly one of the most beautiful she'd ever seen. The valley was filled with the thick fog that had earned the area the Blue Ridge nickname. The mist was a deep purple contrast to the orange-and-pink sky above. Given her awakening overnight to who God truly was, the view was almost like a blessing over her life.

A tug at her hand jerked her back into the present and she moved to tighten her grip on the leash, but it was too late. A squirrel darted across the small clearing and into the woods, and Kito pulled the leash from her hand, disappearing into the trees.

"Not again." Knowing that dog, he'd run straight off the edge of the world when he got to a cliff. She gave chase, running alongside the barn and into the woods at the back. She paused, listening for the sounds of Kito crashing through the brush.

Twigs and leaves rattled to the right.

Macey turned on one heel and started running, but the sight in front of her stopped her feet and her heart.

In a small clearing, illuminated by the early morning sun, a hooded figure appeared, pistol in hand and aimed directly at Macey's heart.

"Can you say that again?" Trey sank into the seat at the kitchen table and glanced out the window. Macey had rounded the corner of the barn with Kito a minute or two earlier, and he had to remind himself she was fairly safe here.

But the words the commander had just said almost made him forget to double-check on her whereabouts.

Leaning back against the island in the kitchen, Captain Harrison crossed his arms. "DNA came back on that sample you collected from the window at Macey's house. It's a near-perfect match. Olivia Whittaker is alive. Either that or she has an identical twin none of us knew about."

Olivia. Alive. The faint scent of coffee hanging in the air was almost enough to nauseate him at this point. This was more than Trey's mind could put together. Running on fumes after being awake for far too long wasn't helping, either. The whole thing was surreal. "She faked her death? How?"

Did he really have to ask? He knew. Already, he knew. Trey drummed his fingers on the table. He should have known all along. "Let me guess. The aunt that Macey has been talking to was either Olivia or someone working with her."

"That'd be my guess."

From the other side of the table came soft clicks as Dana worked at her laptop, searching the videos from the camera at Macey's house with greater urgency than ever. If they could get a video of Olivia actually in the house at some point after her death, they'd have a whole lot more evidence. They could nab what she was searching for and whether or not she'd been able to retrieve it.

At the moment, though, that was Dana's focus. Trey's had to be on Macey. "Macey had no reason to doubt Olivia was dead. She had no one to double-check with. As someone who wasn't even related to her, she wouldn't have been able to get any real information anyway. When an 'aunt' called with the news, what else would she think?" What else would he himself think? He'd bought the ruse, as well. "I should have caught that." Were there any more ways he could fail in the course of this investigation?

"Hindsight's twenty-twenty, brother." Rich clamped a hand on his shoulder, then sat in the chair beside him. "We all missed that."

"I ran it through the databases when you told me she died and came up with a death certificate and an accident report. It isn't a difficult hack to a database to plant just enough evidence to make it look real."

"So there was never a wreck at all?" How far had Olivia gone to cover her tracks?

"There was a real car accident." Commander Harrison scratched his chin, then recrossed his arms and adjusted his stance. "If I had to guess, I'd say Olivia planned to fake her death for a while, either to get out of the game and cover her tracks or to pin everything on Macey, then move on with a life of luxury after her last big sale. There was a car accident with deaths, but the names were never released. I'm thinking she stumbled on that accident and put her plan into place.

Trouble was, she'd left the intel behind and had to find a way to get it."

"Or she figured it was safe at the house until someone else came after it," Rich said.

If Olivia was the one watching the house cameras, she'd know there had been an intrusion. "So the big question is, who's trying to grab Macey? Olivia and an as-yet-unknown crew? Or whoever she's been selling to and didn't deliver to?"

"Or both." Rich had never been accused of being an optimist. Looked like he wasn't about to start now.

Trey shoved away from the table and walked to the window.

Macey still hadn't come back around the corner. Either Kito was taking more time than usual or something was very wrong.

He stepped sideways for the door.

Everyone in the room must have noticed, because both men were on his heels.

"What is it?" Rich stood close behind his right shoulder.

"I'm going to check on Macey." He relayed his concerns, then jogged down the steps, his two teammates on his heels again. "Mace?"

No answer.

His heart rate and his pace picked up. He skidded around the corner and stopped, Rich nearly running into his back when he did.

The wide-open space beside the barn stood empty. No Kito. No Macey.

No clues.

Grinding his teeth together, Trey bit back words he

never said anymore. When he finally found his voice again, it was harsh and ragged. "I never should have left her alone." He whirled toward Captain Harrison. "I thought we were safe here."

"We are. Chances are the dog took off after an animal and she followed."

Trey's pulse rate throttled back. Knowing Kito, that was a very good chance. That dog hauled off after everything that crossed his path. And knowing Macey, she wouldn't have left her dog in the woods alone to run back to the house to give them a status report before searching for him. "Macey!" His voice echoed to him from the nearby rocks and trees.

Silence.

The commander stepped around him and pointed at a slim trail that quickly disappeared into the woods. "I'm thinking this way. If that's the case, she's followed the dog away from the ridge, but it wouldn't take a lot for the two of them to get turned around and lost in the woods around here."

Great. Even more for Trey to worry about. Next thing he knew, someone would bring up black bears and bobcats. There was nothing either of them could say that he hadn't already thought. "She can't have gotten far."

"You go left. Rich, take the right. And I'll barrel straight through. Call when you find her." The commander laid a hand on Trey's shoulder as he passed, trekking into the woods. "We're the only ones around, so she's safe. We'll find her fast. Like you said, she can't have gotten very far." He was several feet into the woods before he called over his shoulder, "Watch where you put your feet down. It's rattlesnake season."

"Rattlesnakes. Great." So there *was* a danger he hadn't thought of. Trey set off into the underbrush, picking his way carefully. The early morning air was relatively cool, and the budding leaves layered varying shades of green among the trees. Any other day he'd relish a hike like this. Today, he couldn't stop the feeling in his gut that said Macey was in serious danger.

"Macey!" He called her name and stopped to listen.

Still nothing. From behind and to his left, Rich and the commander both called her name, their voices growing fainter as they all hiked farther from one another. Why couldn't she hear them? Worse, why wasn't she answering? Visions of her at the bottom of a ravine or faint from a rattlesnake bite all warred with his common sense. *God, I just found her. I can't lose her now.*

A muffled sound came from his left, a consistent thud that sounded way too familiar, and not at all like he needed Macey to sound.

This was a four-legged sound. He reached for the pistol at his hip and rested his hand on it, just in case his hunch was wrong and a bobcat was bearing down on him. "Kito! Come!"

The crashing stopped, but then it picked up with greater intensity. Within seconds, that beautiful husky burst through the underbrush and jumped on Trey, paws on his chest, clearly happy to see a familiar face.

With a burst of relief, Trey rubbed the dog's head. "Good boy. I mean, bad boy for running away, but good boy for coming when I called you. Where's Macey?" He wrapped the leash around his hand and looked in the direction from which Kito had appeared, expecting to see Macey right behind him.

But the only sight was trees and rocks. The only sound the birds who were greeting the dawn.

Macey was still missing. And the longer she was gone, the more likely it became that he might have lost her forever.

SIXTEEN

"I don't have what you want. I promise." Macey's eyes refused to leave the gun aimed at her. Her hands went out to her sides, away from her body. She'd never routinely carried a weapon in her life, but somehow she had to show this person she was unarmed. "Please." She couldn't die out here. Trey and his team would never know which way she'd followed Kito. She could vanish into these woods and no one would ever be able to find her.

The figure stepped closer and out of the shadows, weapon steady.

Macey forced her brain into defense mode. She could get out of this. There had to be a way to defend herself. She'd trained for this over the years.

But so far, there was nothing. As though the person knew her strengths, they stayed at a distance where their gun would be effective but Macey's training would not.

The gunman shifted to the side again, widening their stance.

There was something familiar about the gait, about

the stance, about the build… Something she should know, should recognize. Macey dragged her gaze from the gun to the head.

With their free hand, the stranger reached up and swept the hood back. Jet-black hair tumbled out and surrounded a face that—

The force of recognition shook the air from Macey's lungs. "Olivia." The name came out on what felt like her last breath. Her former roommate and friend had dyed her blond hair, but there was no doubt whose face it was.

Except Macey had never seen Olivia's expression the way it was today, hard and desperate. "I want Kito. Where is he?"

"What?" This was about her dog? Olivia had come back from the dead and was holding her at gunpoint over her dog? "Why?"

"Because what I need is on a microchip in his neck." Olivia steadied the weapon in a way that was entirely too practiced and stepped threateningly closer to Macey. "You tell me where he is, I take him, and you walk away. Promise."

Lord, please let Kito have made his way back to the house, somewhere safe where Olivia can't get to him. Please. There was no doubt Olivia's promises were empty. There was no doubt that once she had Kito, she'd likely kill them both. No way would someone who had set up such an elaborate scheme to frame Macey leave a witness alive. "You're lying."

Arching an eyebrow, Olivia looked Macey up and down. "You're stronger than you used to be, aren't you? Something about your friendship with Trey maybe?" Her smile was tight and mean, like a bully taunting the weak kid at school. "You know he's not really your friend. He's investigating you. Looking to put you in prison for the rest of your life."

Macey pulled herself taller. Olivia had no idea how much Macey knew, which meant she might not realize her plan had been fully uncovered. Something deep inside her refused to back down to a common bully, even if that bully was holding a pistol in a deadly steady grip. "Trey's the good guy, not you."

Olivia blinked rapidly, her arm dropping slightly before she raised it again. "He already told you?"

"Everything."

Where was this boldness coming from? It definitely wasn't from her. Somehow, Macey had stepped outside of herself. Maybe it was because she'd experienced the worst sort of betrayal from this woman and Olivia couldn't hurt her any deeper. Maybe it was because she'd surrendered her life to God's authority and had no fear of death. Regrets, but not fear.

She had no idea where her peace originated. She only knew Olivia didn't scare her.

But Olivia sure was scared. It showed in the furrow of her forehead and in the deep V between her brows. "Jeffrey said this would work. It *will* work. You're lying." Uncertainty crept into the bravado, wavering her voice and the pistol in her hand. "I want the dog. Now."

"He's in the woods somewhere, chasing a squirrel. You'll have to find him."

Something in Olivia seemed to reset. With her free hand, she pulled her phone from her pocket and glanced at the screen. "You think I can't? How do you think I found you? There's a tracker in his collar. When I saw on the video that someone had broken in looking for the intel, I tried to come and get him, but Trey's gotten in the way every time. Killing a military investigator to get to the dog would have set off a world of people looking for me. It's one thing to murder a civilian and another entirely to kill a federal agent. We're going to find Kito, and then, sadly, it's going to look like you shot him and then yourself because you're so devastated over what you've done to your country."

For the first time, fear skittered along Macey's spine. Olivia could do what she wanted to her, but she couldn't touch Kito. He was an innocent animal. She dug her teeth into her lip and prayed for Trey to realize she was gone, for Captain Harrison and Rich and him to come bursting into the clearing to save her. *Please.*

"Start walking." Olivia glanced at her phone, then waved the gun to the left. "That way. I can get him within half a mile, and he's somewhere to our left, back toward the house. If you run, I'll put a bullet in your back and forget the suicide angle."

Lord, keep Kito far away. Honestly, she didn't care what happened to her. She wanted her dog to be safe. Macey started walking, stomping through the underbrush, praying Trey or someone on his team would hear her and realize something was wrong.

A rustle in the underbrush paralyzed her foot above the ground.

Olivia stopped walking behind her, likely leveling her pistol at the sound.

Not Kito. Please not Kito.

Two birds beat the air with their wings and soared into the trees.

Macey dared a glance over her shoulder at Olivia, who shifted the weapon toward her back and was watching her with deadly intent. "Keep walking." She glanced at her phone screen and gestured to the left. "He's around here somewhere."

"You might as well tell me everything if you're going to kill me. Give me the dignity of knowing why I'm going to die." Macey stepped carefully over a fallen branch. If only she was fast enough to pick it up and swing it, but Olivia seemed comfortable with that pistol and would likely pull the trigger before Macey could wrap her fingers around any makeshift weapon.

"Not much to tell." Olivia had always been a little bit of a braggart, a little bit cocky about her job in intelligence. "I don't have an aunt. You've been in contact with me all along. You should have done your homework. Don't believe everything you read. Turns out, with no living relatives, it's not so hard to fake your death. The only person I really needed to fool was you. And I had Jeff's people do just enough to make it look like I really did die. Enough to fool the government, anyway. Same people helped him fake his death."

"He double-crossed his brother, didn't he?"

"You're catching on. The intel I dug up can take down our military piece by piece. It's a vulnerability in the system that allows access to the communications channels. Whoever has the knowledge of that back door can pass any word officially through any channel that they want. An order to fight, an order to stand down... It could cause chaos. No one would know who to trust. Bidding for that kind of intel goes high. And rather than let Sapphire Skull use it to fund themselves, we figured we could retire somewhere together in style."

"Were those your men in my house?"

Olivia laughed. "Nope. They're with Sapphire. They think you're the leak. They think you have what they want. I was on retainer to them, a monthly stipend, if you will. And they found out I was holding back something big. Only, all along, I've let them think I was you. There was a dummy drive in the photo on my dresser, and that kept them busy for a few days, but once they figured that out, they came after you again, wanting what they'd paid for."

She chuckled. "And you had it all along. I tried to get into the house the other night, but Trey was there. Since Sapphire was clearly onto you, I figured I'd bide my time and they'd kill you eventually. Then I'd just scoop up Kito and move on. When I saw the in-house video, I figured out Trey knew you were innocent, but by the time I got to the house, they were already in the process of moving you. Fortunately, you brought the collar along, and here we are."

The bushes rustled again. Three more birds flushed out of the brush, flying toward the risen sun.

"Stupid birds," Olivia muttered. She jabbed the pistol into Macey's spine. "Walk."

She was so close. Too close. A mistake too many attackers made. Without stopping to think what she was doing, relying solely on instinct and training, Macey ducked and spun, driving her shoulder into Olivia's stomach. She shoved Olivia backward against a tree and the two of them dropped to the ground. The gun fired wildly, then clattered into the leaves beside them and disappeared in the thick tangle.

Olivia countered with a blow to Macey's sternum, driving the air from her chest.

Before Macey could fight back, Olivia straddled her chest and wrapped her hands around Macey's throat. "You shouldn't have taught me how to fight back." She squeezed tighter. "You're too much trouble."

Macey struggled and fought, digging her nails into Olivia's wrists, trying to pull free. Her pulse pounded in her head. Her windpipe ached. She couldn't breathe. Couldn't focus. Couldn't hear anything outside of the pounding in her ears.

Blackness came quickly, tingeing the edges of the world and narrowing on the hatred in Olivia's eyes as she choked the life away from her.

Another sound, so far away. A blur of something through the darkness.

Suddenly, Olivia's weight was gone.

Macey struggled for air and fought to roll away, to sit up, to get moving.

But another shadow blocked the morning sunlight. She forced her eyes open.

Kito. He stood over her, looking down with his giant doggy face. She lifted a hand, wrapped her fingers in his neck fur, and the world went black.

Trey paced the deck, watching the activity in the driveway and wondering how hard it would be to take down Captain Harrison, who blocked the door to the house.

Without taking his eyes off the vehicles in the driveway, the commander said, "Sit down, Blackburn. You're making me nervous."

He glared at his commander. The man had nothing to be nervous about. The woman he loved wasn't inside the house right now, being looked over by medics. He hadn't carried Macey out of the woods, half-conscious with bruises already forming around her neck. He hadn't witnessed a known criminal with her hands wrapped around the throat of—

"Stop reliving it. It won't do anything but raise your blood pressure. She was conscious by the time the medics got here. They'll let you in soon."

Trey walked to the deck rail and spread his hands wide, leaning heavily on the wood. Almost too many vehicles to count flooded the open area around the house and partially blocked the drive. A convoy of SUVs had already left and more were pulling out behind them, hauling Olivia into custody. She'd face more questioning than she'd ever dreamed. And, hopefully, she'd give them enough to shut the Fryes and Sapphire Skull down for good.

She'd better count her blessings that Trey wasn't doing the questioning. His adrenaline and anger still ran high. He'd raced with Kito toward the sound of a gunshot, terrified of what he'd find. When he'd come upon that small clearing and seen Olivia's hands around Macey's neck, he'd never known such rage.

But Kito had only seen his long-lost mistress. He'd pulled free from Trey's grasp and rushed at the woman, knocking her sideways.

Trey had used that advantage and managed to get her

on the ground and cuffed just as the rest of his team ran up, alerted by the same shot he'd followed.

They hauled Olivia out while he ran to Macey, terrified he was too late. Her neck was so red. Her face was so lifeless... But she'd come around as he'd carried her to the house, the commander calling in help as they made their way back. Medics from nearby Camp McGee were already waiting and had rushed Macey, who'd been trying to talk, away from him and inside, barring him entry.

He wanted to know, needed to know, that she was okay. And they wouldn't let him in. Like he was the failure. Like he'd let this happen. Like he was no better than his old—

No. Trey lifted his shoulders and pulled his hands from the rail. He wasn't his old self. Like he'd told Macey, he was a new person. Those men were doing their job and there was no room for him to start doubting what he knew to be true about his life in Christ. He was a man who was competent and capable and could be trusted. A man who—

Behind him, the door opened, and he whirled around. The taller of the two medics who had whisked Macey inside stepped out and Trey was in front of her before she could shut the door. "How is she?"

Behind him, Captain Harrison chuckled.

Trey didn't care. He could laugh all he wanted. Macey was what mattered, not what anyone else thought of him.

The female medic gave Trey an understanding smile. "Fortunately for her, Olivia Whittaker didn't learn her self-defense very well. She choked off Macey Price's carotid instead of crushing her windpipe. Painful and causing a loss of consciousness but probably not doing permanent damage." She looked over Trey's shoulder at the commander. "She's refusing transport. I'd advise getting her to a hospital for some scans to be certain, but she seems to be fine. She'll bruise, and it will look horrible, but I'm cautiously optimistic there's no permanent damage."

Trey didn't wait to hear more. He pushed into the house, where the male medic was packing a case at the kitchen table. "Where is she?"

The man aimed a finger at the living room.

Macey was propped up on the couch. She smiled weakly when she saw Trey. "Where'd you disappear to?"

"They barred the door. Wouldn't let me in. I fought with all I had, but there were more of them than there was of me."

"I know you better than that." Her smile widened. "They ordered you to stay outside, so you did."

Yeah, she knew him, all right. Better than anyone else in the world ever had. He stepped around the recliner and walked over to the couch, dropping to his knees on the hardwood beside Kito, who lay protectively on the floor by Macey. "How do you feel?"

"Like someone tried to kill me." She lifted her hand and laid it on the back of his neck. "But better now that you're here."

"You took her down, huh?"

"I fought hard. Almost won, too. Turns out I'm a good teacher and she used my knowledge against me." She glanced past him. "So Kito saved the day."

"Of course he did. He's a good dog like that."

At the sound of his name, Kito raised his head and shoved his nose against Trey's knee. *Pet me.*

Macey smiled. "Sometimes, I think he likes you better than he likes me."

"Never. Nobody could ever love anyone more than they love you." He purposely threw the word out there, testing the waters, wondering if she could read his mind the way he'd read hers before.

Dropping her hand to the side of the couch, Macey scratched Kito's head close to where Trey's hand rested. She arched an eyebrow. "This is true love. You think this happens every day?"

Trey rolled his eyes and laughed. That movie again. The one that had actually saved their lives. He'd love it—and her—for the rest of his days. And if he was going to make the leap, he might as well go all the way. "You'll probably play the theme song for that movie in the prelude of our wedding, won't you?"

Without a breath of hesitation, Macey leaned forward until her nose practically brushed his. "Definitely."

This time, she kissed him. And when she did, every doubt, every fear and every question of whether or not he was worthy of her love vanished. This was his gift and his future…and he would thank God for it every day for the rest of his life.

EPILOGUE

It was entirely too hot outside. And entirely too muggy.

Trey grabbed the sides of his pickup truck's bed, planted his feet and leaned back to stretch the tight muscles in his shoulders. He'd mowed Macey's grass early to avoid the heat, but he'd still finished up dusty and gross. The scent of fresh-cut grass hung in the air. Usually, he loved the summer smell, but today it only reminded him of misery.

Whoever had scheduled moving day for the inferno heat of July needed a serious talking-to. Getting out of the North Carolina Sandhills in the heat of summer couldn't happen fast enough. He was ready for his beloved mountains.

And the start of his new life.

A door slammed shut and Trey pulled himself straight.

On the front porch, Macey stopped and surveyed the front yard with Kito at her side. A blue bucket full of cleaning supplies dangled loosely from her fingers, and she reached down and scratched the dog's head with her free hand. Her hair was pulled back from her face, and she wore cutoff jean shorts and one of Trey's old PT shirts, streaked with house dust and grime. Macey looked exactly like a woman who'd been cleaning an empty house in the worst part of a North Carolina summer.

And she'd never been more beautiful.

Trey gave her a moment to reflect, then knocked his knuckles against the hot metal of the truck. If they didn't get moving, he'd stand here all day and watch her. It had become his favorite pastime. "You about ready to roll? I'm ready for some AC and the biggest sweet tea they can pass me through a drive-through window. Maybe even two of them."

She turned his way with a grin. "You're speaking my language. Let me give Kito one more run in the backyard before we head out." With a final pat to the dog's head, she practically jumped down the stairs, wiping a rogue hair from her eyes. The diamond on her left hand caught the midday July sun and sparkled like runway lights.

The beacon that called him home. Yeah, he was definitely ready to get moving on their new life. The time between the securing of Macey's freedom in the fall and this day in the summer had been long. Even longer since he'd dropped to one knee on Valentine's Day and asked her to wear that ring. He'd created a cliché right down to the twinkly lights he'd twined around the railing on her deck, and she'd loved every second of it, especially since her name had officially been cleared and her nightmare had officially been declared over just the day before.

Once in custody, Olivia had poured out everything,

and her testimony had been more than enough to locate the Frye brothers and to shut down Sapphire Skull for good. With the destruction of their terroristic plans, Macey was finally free to live her life in safety.

With Trey.

He followed her to the back gate, where they both stood and stared at the yard he'd mowed that morning. The new owners would take possession of the house the next day. "You locked up?"

"Yep."

"You sad to leave it?" Trey braced his hands on the rough wood fence. It had been the one worry that had nagged him ever since she'd accepted his proposal. Being away from her while he worked at Camp McGee often swamped him with doubts. He'd had more than one marathon prayer session with Jesus, working out his trust issues and his fears.

Macey wasn't going to betray him, he had no doubt. But she was leaving everything for him: her home, her job, her entire life… It seemed as though she was doing all of the sacrificing.

"I'm not sad at all. I'm definitely not going to miss a house where everywhere I turn, all I see is Olivia's betrayal and the place where armed men busted in my door. Or where I shot a man inside my own home." Shuddering, Macey rested her head against his shoulder. "Besides, since you left in January, what reason do I have to stay?"

"Your job?"

"Found a better one." Macey had taken on a new position at the clinic on Camp McGee, heading up their physical therapy department. She'd be perfect with the soldiers recovering there.

"Your family?" He couldn't help pushing. Maybe there was a part of him that still needed to hear her say he was the love of her life. He smiled and kissed her on top of the head. Yeah, he'd never get tired of hearing that.

"God will work that out." As she was. Although she was working to reconnect with her mother, the going was rough and a matter of constant prayer. She tilted her head and kissed his jaw. "Besides, we're building one together. But what about you? You're giving up the bachelor life and you're also giving up undercover work. You good with that?"

When Kito took off after a bird, Trey put his arm around Macey's shoulders. He was more than good with that. His stint working Macey's case had convinced him that he wasn't cut out for pretending to be someone and something he wasn't. After a few long talks with his chain of command and a whole lot of prayer, Trey had decided to take on a new assignment, coordinating and supporting the undercover operatives who were out in the field. "I'm perfectly good with that." He squeezed her shoulder. "Keeps me home more with you."

Macey shifted beneath his arm, turned and wrapped her arms around his neck. "I'm perfectly good with that, too."

Trey slipped his arms around her waist and clasped his hands at her lower back, then lowered his head to kiss her.

She met him halfway.

The same way she would in two days, when they

were presented for the first time as husband and wife at an open-air chapel in the mountains near Camp McGee.

And when Trey stood before everyone and proved that God had not only restored his past… He'd given Trey a greater future than he ever could have imagined.

* * * * *

If you enjoyed this story,
look for these other books by Jodie Bailey:

Mistaken Twin
Hidden Twin
Fatal Identity

Dear Reader,

The foundation of Trey and Macey's story is rooted in Isaiah 41:10. While I was writing their story, my family's life was thrown totally off-kilter by two unexpected twists…and that was before COVID-19 came along to make everything even more difficult. It has been a season of tears and fears and stresses. It has also been a season of miracles that I will never be able to explain. Through it all—the very good days and the horribly rough days—we have seen evidence of God's presence. I wish I had the time to sit down and tell you all of the ways God has definitely not left us nor forsaken us.

We've all been hurt. Some of us, like Trey, have had our lives stung by betrayal. Others, like Macey, have felt the devastation of abandonment. Those things leave scars that last, even after the pain has dulled. It's so easy to project the traits of fallible humans onto God. It's so easy to believe the lie that He would walk away.

But I promise you, He doesn't. And like I've said in reader letters before, when we look back, we can see exactly where He was and that He was there all along. In people… In places… In the little "coincidences" that pop up. In a moment of peace amid a storm. I beg you to look for Him. I promise you will find Him.

If you'd like, drop by www.jodiebailey.com and say hello. I'd love to hear from you. I'd especially love to hear about those times God has shown you His presence. Those stories are my very favorite.

Jodie Bailey

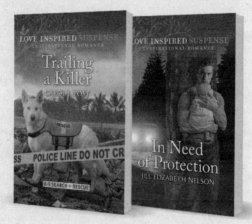

COMING NEXT MONTH FROM
Love Inspired Suspense

Available March 9, 2021

MOUNTAIN SURVIVAL
K-9 Search and Rescue • by Christy Barritt
When search-and-rescue park ranger Autumn Mercer and her K-9 partner, Sherlock, meet a stranger in the mountains whose brother has gone missing, they drop everything to join the search. But with a storm and gunmen closing in, can she and Derek Peterson survive long enough to complete their mission?

FRAMED IN DEATH VALLEY
Desert Justice • by Dana Mentink
Released from jail after being framed for murder, Beckett Duke returns home to find his wife pregnant—with a target on her back. Though he's determined to shield Laney from an unknown enemy, he broke her heart when he'd asked for a divorce after his arrest. Can he convince her to trust him with her life?

HIDDEN AMISH SECRETS
by Debby Giusti
Julianne Graber left her Amish life behind after a family tragedy, but now she's back to sell the family home—and someone's dead set on getting rid of her. With her neighbor William Lavy by her side, Julianne must uncover deadly secrets to make sense of the past *and* present...even if it kills her.

DEADLY RIVER PURSUIT
by Heather Woodhaven
After rafting guide Nora Radley witnesses her staff member's murder—and narrowly escapes being shot—the crime scene casts doubt on her story. Only her ex-fiancé, law enforcement ranger Henry McKnight, believes her. But as they find connections to a ten-year-old cold case, the killer will do anything to silence them both.

TEXAS TARGET STANDOFF
Cowboy Lawmen • by Virginia Vaughan
In the crosshairs of a sniper, military psychologist Shelby Warren turns to navy SEAL Paul Avery for protection. Paul's not about to let Shelby get gunned down in front of him. He needs her evaluation to get back to his team...and rescuing her might finally give him the redemption he's been searching for.

ABDUCTED IN ALASKA
by Darlene L. Turner
Saving a boy who has escaped his captors puts Canadian border patrol officer Hannah Morgan right into the path of a ruthless child-smuggling ring. With help from police constable Layke Jackson, can she keep the child safe—and stay alive—while working to stop the gang from endangering more children?

LOOK FOR THESE AND OTHER LOVE INSPIRED BOOKS WHEREVER BOOKS ARE SOLD, INCLUDING MOST BOOKSTORES, SUPERMARKETS, DISCOUNT STORES AND DRUGSTORES.

LISCNM0221

SPECIAL EXCERPT FROM

LOVE INSPIRED SUSPENSE
INSPIRATIONAL ROMANCE

*When search-and-rescue park ranger Autumn Mercer
and her K-9 partner, Sherlock, meet a stranger in the
mountains whose brother has gone missing, they drop
everything to join the search. But with a storm and
gunmen closing in, can she and Derek Peterson survive
long enough to complete their mission?*

Read on for a sneak preview of
Mountain Survival *by Christy Barritt,*
available March 2021 from Love Inspired Suspense.

After another bullet whizzed by, Autumn turned, trying
to get a better view of the gunman. She had to figure out
where he was.

"Stay behind the tree," she whispered to Derek. "And
keep an eye on Sherlock."

Finally, she spotted a gunman crouched behind a
nearby boulder. The front of his Glock was pointed at her.

A Glock? The man definitely wasn't a hunter.

Autumn already knew that, though.

Hunters didn't aim their guns at people.

Her gaze continued to scan the area. She spotted
another man behind a tree and a third man behind another
boulder.

Who were these guys? And what did they want from
Autumn?

Backup couldn't get here soon enough.

The breeze picked up again, bringing another smattering of rain with it. They didn't have much time here. The conditions were going to become perilous at any minute. The storm might drive the gunman away, but it would present other dangers in the process.

She spotted a fourth man behind another tree in the distance. They all surrounded the campsite where Derek and his brother had set up.

They'd been waiting for Derek to return, hadn't they?

Why? What sense did that make?

She didn't have time to think about that now. Another bullet came flying past, piercing a nearby tree.

"What are we going to do?" Derek whispered. "Can I help?"

"Just stay behind a tree and remain quiet," she said. "We don't want to make this too easy for them."

Sherlock let out a little whine, but Autumn shushed the dog.

The man fired again. This time the bullet split the wood only inches from her.

Autumn's heart raced. These men were out for blood.

Even if the men ran out of bullets, she and Derek were going to be outnumbered. They couldn't just wait here for that to happen.

She had to act—and now.

She turned, pulling her gun's trigger.

Don't miss
Mountain Survival *by Christy Barritt,*
available March 2021 wherever Love Inspired Suspense
books and ebooks are sold.

LoveInspired.com

LOVE INSPIRED
INSPIRATIONAL ROMANCE

UPLIFTING STORIES OF FAITH, FORGIVENESS AND HOPE.

Join our social communities to connect with other readers who share your love!

Sign up for the Love Inspired newsletter at **LoveInspired.com** to be the first to find out about upcoming titles, special promotions and exclusive content.

CONNECT WITH US AT:

Facebook.com/LoveInspiredBooks

Twitter.com/LoveInspiredBks

Facebook.com/groups/HarlequinConnection